bella

Other Novels by Lisa Samson

Embrace Me

Quaker Summer

Straight Up

The Church Ladies

Tiger Lillie

Club Sandwich

The Living End

Women's Intuition

Songbird

bella

A Novelization of the Award-Winning Movie

Novelization by Lisa Samson

Screenplay by Alejandro Monteverde, Patrick Million, and Leo Severino

THOMAS NELSON
Since 1798

NASHVILLE   DALLAS   MEXICO CITY   RIO DE JANEIRO   BEIJING

Dedication from Lisa:
For Leigh Heller, who loves life

Published in Nashville, Tennessee, by Thomas Nelson. Thomas Nelson is a registered trademark of Thomas Nelson, Inc.

Thomas Nelson books may be purchased in bulk for educational, business, fund-raising, or sales promotional use. For information, please e-mail SpecialMarkets@ThomasNelson.com.

Publisher's Note: This novel is a work of fiction. Names, characters, places, and incidents are either products of the author's imagination or used fictitiously. All characters are fictional, and any similarity to people living or dead is purely coincidental.

Because subtitles aren't appropriate for fiction, all words spoken by a character in Spanish will be italicized in English.

Library of Congress Cataloging-in-Publication Data

Samson, Lisa, 1964–
  Bella : a novelization of the award-winning movie / by Lisa Samson.
    p. cm.
  ISBN 1-59554-608-1 (softcover) 1. Pregnant women—Fiction.
2. Abortion—Fiction. 3. Mexican Americans—Fiction. 4. Psychological fiction. I. Title.
  PS3569.A46673B46 2008
  813'.54—dc22   2008009407

Printed in the United States of America
08 09 10 11 12 RRD 5 4 3 2 1

Prologue

Nobody expected it to happen to them personally, and with the way the population of the planet kept increasing, that seemed a little silly. Nina could hardly believe she was no different in that regard. So much for all those corny kids' shows that told her, over and over again, how "special" she was.

Yeah. Special.

Right.

Nina rubbed her hands together in her lap, warming them between her knees despite the warm spring day outside. The paneled wall, cheap paneling like her next-door neighbor had in his club basement when she was growing up, cast a satin glow from the anemic fluorescent strip lights. And those awful plastic chairs! In rows much less, as if what she was about to do was a privilege and not a right, something you just shut up and got in line for, thankful that people were willing to help out in your time of need.

Didn't these people know she'd need more than some outdated sterility at a time like this? What was wrong with them? They sounded so caring on the phone; they sounded pink and lacy and seventy-five degrees, at least.

Guess the money in her pocket wouldn't be going for décor. Or heat.

She felt so cold. Shivering, she took stock of the occupants in the waiting room, two couples and two other women just as alone as she. One looked through a newsmagazine; the other looked at the floor. They all sat in their respective bubbles, everybody knowing why the others came. But for some, this was a secret they'd take to their graves. It was almost as if they could hear each other's hearts breaking.

He said he'd come and she'd trusted him. But it was almost time to go in. She was pretty sure these folks maintained a sort of super-punctuality, lest someone have second thoughts and beat it out of there. And he'd yet to arrive.

Figures. Pieter let her down. Why not José too?

No, that wasn't fair. José wasn't at all like Pieter. Everybody at the restaurant thought José was a little crazy. But today she knew better.

Finally, he rushed through the door, her new friend bringing a fresh wind in with him.

He sat down next to her and took her hands, his shadowy blue eyes rimmed with dark lashes. "I'm sorry I'm late." He came close and whispered in her ear, his breath warm, smelling of mouthwash. "Let me help you. Please, Nina." And he whispered something else in his comforting Latino accent, but she couldn't hear it, for the nurse had called her name.

She arose. José steadied her as her knees buckled; she touched his shoulder and tried to smile as he reached out, embracing her. Then she followed the broad back of the nurse whose surgical scrubs were, ironically, printed with kittens. Nina looked up through the ceiling to the sky. Kittens. Did it have to be kittens?

She looked over her shoulder as the door to the hallway outside the surgical suite closed. José was pulling rosary beads out of his pocket. A rosary? In this place? And yet she took comfort in his prayers.

So she stripped down to nothing, feeling more naked than she ever had before, shrugged into the hospital gown, and waited for what seemed like all the years she'd lived in that city. She lay flat on the table, staring up at the ceiling, tears filling her eyes, and hoping, like millions of other women had hoped before her, this would make everything go away and tomorrow life would return to normal.

She curled her hands into fists, eyeing her bag of clothing by the changing room door.

One

The week before.

José journeyed to the cemetery like he did most mornings. He stood by the grave, the words of his grandmother filling his mind as the breeze of early morning filled his nose and lungs.

"If you want to make God laugh, tell him your plans."

And there wasn't a day that went by that José didn't live with those words floating in his mind like a white gull circling by the sea, gently reminding him of the four years spent on Riker's Island.

Newborn leaves shivered on the cherry trees that lined the lanes of the cemetery.

Oh yes. He'd had plans. As a boy on a horse ranch in Mexico, he knew exactly what he wanted to be, but nothing turned out as he'd planned. It never did. Life took you right to the edge of where you wanted to go, then turned left. There were only a few people in the world he knew who did exactly what they wanted with their lives. Unfortunately, they were his mother, his father, and his older brother, Manny.

But everyone else? No. Most of them seemed to be scratching along like him, working a job there in the city, acting a part, and wondering what the world would hold if they weren't tied down by their mistakes.

"You're such a good-looking boy," that same grandmother had always told him as he was growing up. But nobody in the courtroom that day cared whether or not he was handsome. He was guilty, and they threw him into prison. Each day José realized he'd gotten off easy compared to the person he killed. Four years was nothing.

In front of the granite headstone, the grass was now overgrown, the tender spring shoots mingling with last year's dried blades, and he knelt and crossed himself, hoping somehow the pictures in his mind constituted a prayer. The scene that day ran across his mind again, and he prayed for God to suspend time and run it backward. But God didn't work that way that he ever could tell.

Time to go to work. He traced the name with his fingertips, then laid some flowers in front of the small tombstone.

He stood up, brushing the grass from his jeans. The pink

of the roses bled into the green of the grave-grass as the spring wind and the grief he nurtured watered his eyes.

José skirted the graves and hurried down the lanes of the city cemetery, through the iron gates, toward the subway station. He could make this walk blindfolded after the past two years of pilgrimage.

The sun was rising, not looking down on him, but peering through alleys and over fences. José broke into a fast walk. He didn't realize he'd stayed by the grave so long. Manny would be furious if the kitchen wasn't running smoothly. And Manny got what he wanted: success, good horses, and, well, maybe not his share of women, but he didn't have time for them anyway. The two brothers were nothing alike. It made sense. But it didn't make working for him any easier.

He already had the staff dinner in mind when he unlocked the door, flipped on the lights, and heated up the ovens. He could feed people. Keep them alive for another day. This he could do.

And so he cooked, chopped and stirred, tasted and plated, each day, all day—the heat of the kitchen drawing out his sweat. It rolled into his eyes making them smart, and José let Manny yell and make fusses because he knew he deserved a lifetime of penance. And this penance wasn't given to him by his priest; it was given to him by God. Or rather that was what José had come to believe.

Two

She'd been nauseated for two weeks now. Every morning, there she'd be: head over the toilet, the smell of porcelain mixing with toilet water, not heavy and overpowering like one of the restrooms near the beach in Atlantic City, but that smell a person can't scrub away no matter how forcefully you swish the brush each week.

And those faint smells seemed to grow under the weight of a stomach so upset, even the thought of lasagna or fried fish, let alone bathroom odors, buckled it in two.

Crackers.

Nina grabbed a sleeve of saltines, devoured three, and headed out the door, down the steps, and into the midmorning street. At least it was springtime, and a warm one at that. She shoved her sweater into her large, backpack-style purse. Nina loved spring.

She was born in the spring. However, her birthday a week ago, the big two-five, could have well been the most depressing day of her life. Cassie, her best friend from high school, just had her first child, and of course she called, a fake trill in her voice when she talked about Nina living an exciting life, single in the city, trying to make a go of it in the arts, and how many people have that kind of dedication to keep going against all odds, that kind of stick-to-it-ive-ness? Amazing.

The boy who had grown up in the house next door had the same birthday and was in his second year of law school. Ryan e-mailed her like he always did, and she thought maybe she'd invite him out for a drink after she was done waiting tables at El Callejon. *The Alley.*

If all alleys were as nice as El Callejon, New York would be a better place, that was for sure. She'd been mugged once, been twice relieved of her purse, and here she remained in the city that slept with one eye open.

Waiting tables. Renting videos. Eating cheap take-out. Great life, Nina. Great life.

She set her jaw, clipping down the sidewalk in the heavily embroidered waitress uniform, flowers in a prism of colors wending across the black cotton fabric of her full skirt and shirt. At least she worked at an upscale restaurant where they fed their employees dinner before they hit the carpet, trying their best to keep Manny happy or simply to keep away from Manny altogether.

Nina checked her watch and stepped up her pace. She'd wanted to go to the pharmacy, return home, and shower, but she was going to be later than she thought. Nobody told her how tired women in her condition became. For the past week she'd felt as if she'd put in five back-to-back double shifts.

I need this job.

Okay, she could have worked at any restaurant, but she liked it at El Callejon. The staff was her family. Amelia would fold her into her big arms when she was downhearted, bring her homemade sweets on special holidays, show her pictures of her kids. Carlos told the funniest stories of his life in Cuba, then Miami. The man made communism a comedy, but every once in a while he'd let the veil drop and she saw the sadness of leaving a family behind. He and his wife invited her over for Christmas dinners, his kids crawling all over her as she played with them, helping them put together their new toys. Marco said little, but his eyes twinkled when he handed her a plate. Pepito, always listening to sports on his little transistor radio and yelling good-naturedly at the announcers. Margarita, fellow waitress, prettier than she realized and as sweet as Amelia's cookies. Sometimes they'd hang out at each others' apartments, playing Scrabble or Boggle so Nina could help her with her English.

And then there was Pieter. Well, she could leave him behind in a heartbeat. Especially now.

She entered the drugstore a block away from her apartment, shouldered past the people at the register, down aisle three beyond the hair gel, the teeth whitening gel, and the shower gel, and finally stood before the pregnancy tests, all five hundred varieties in their tidy, cheerful little boxes.

Had sex with Pieter been worth this?

No way. She'd had too much to drink at a party he hosted at his house; she stayed late, drank some more, and then, well, it happened. "Get drunk enough and lonely enough and anybody will do," a friend once told her. She didn't believe him, but now she realized he was right. Nina hadn't been out with anybody for over a year. And when Pieter wanted to hook up again, she'd said yes.

She still couldn't figure out why, and she chided herself over and over again.

Was Pieter at all serious about her? No, and he never pretended to be. He didn't want a child with her, and even if he did, Pieter would be a lousy father. The question was, did *she* want a child with him?

Of course not. Not even a little bit. He'd be too hard on the kid when he showed up. He was always at the restaurant sucking up to the boss man. She'd have to teach the kid to throw a baseball, and she had no athletic skills whatsoever. She'd have to help him with math, and she never could solve an equation.

A lousy father, she thought and reached out toward one of the boxes. *A lousy mother too.*

Fabulous combo there, Nina.

She picked up one box and set it down. Looked too complicated. The next, violet with big pink bubbles and how fun! Yippee!

Oh yeah, that's right. She tapped the box against her fingers. Some people actually hoped for a positive result. They'd be standing right where she was with eager faces soaking in all the colors because they'd been trying, you see; they'd been taking their temperatures to see if they were ovulating. They weren't praying every time they went to the bathroom that they'd wipe and come up with bloody toilet paper.

Well, she was tired of that sort of stress. Best to get it over with.

She approached the counter, waiting while an older man in a yellow canvas jacket and plaid pants paid for a cup of stale coffee and a bag of little chocolate donuts, and she smiled at him. Nina always smiled at people who looked sad and a little at odds with walking around, breathing, eating, and sleeping. She knew they had a lot in common.

He exited with a tip of his cap, recognizing her as part of the club. Good. At least there was that.

Wishing to goodness she had on a wedding ring, she handed the bubbly pink test kit to Carla, the clerk. She would make it seem like a happy time, and she wouldn't be pegged as a person who would sleep with just anyone. She wasn't that type of person, but Carla couldn't know that. Nina would bet a lot of money that if Carla had kids, she had them well within the bonds of matrimony. Sure, it seemed that society was more favorable to single mothers these days. Until you found out you were pregnant, and then—whoa!—you felt the stigma down to the soles of your feet. True, nobody kicked you out of the village for immorality anymore; these days you just felt stupid for not looking after your birth control a little more closely.

Where was that guidance counselor who told her to wait "until you're ready" to have sex with a man? Why did Ms. Farley never complete the equation of male + female = quite possibly another male or female, depending on which chromosome came from the male that day? Another male or female who would be totally dependent on you? Who, all eight pounds of them, could take over every bit of your life? *Ready?* What waitress, who didn't have big plans and wasn't married, who didn't even have a guy around worth marrying, was *ready?* Yes, Ms. Farley, how about at least paying for the pregnancy test kit? How about that?

"That'll be $12.63," Carla said. Carla had been work-ing here for years. She gave Nina a half smile. Nina didn't blame her for not revealing the other half. Who wanted to be stuck in a drugstore on a day like today?

Nina riffled through her bag. Wallet, wallet, wallet. Where was it?

Oh no! On the coffee table. She'd shoved it in the back pocket of her jeans last night when she ran down here, to this store, to get a bottle of aspirin. And then she'd taken it out when she got back home and had laid it right by the novel she was reading.

She looked up. "I can't believe this . . . I think I left my wallet at home."

Nina dug into her skirt pocket, pulling out a few tips she had shoved in there the night before—a couple of ones, some change. Carla looked anxiously over Nina's shoulder where a line continued to form.

Behind her, another old man cleared his throat. She looked back at him. What was this, the old man conven-tion? No little chocolate donuts this time, though.

"Can I come back and pay you later? I live close by."

"I know you do. It's okay. You're good for it. My shift is over at four."

"Thanks."

You're good for it. Always a nice thing to hear when you feel your life is proving otherwise.

Nina slid the kit into her bag and hurried back around the corner against the flow of pedestrian traffic and saw herself, a woman wearing huge embroidered flowers, parting the waters in a sea of dark, serious suits. She ran up the steps to her apartment.

She should have been at work two minutes ago.

But nothing else mattered, nothing but knowing the truth. Well, knowing it for sure. If that was even possible.

Three

The paper butterfly lay on the pebbly concrete of the back walk, its wings rising toward the clearest sky the summer had yet to hold. Celia picked it up, its moon-green wings vibrating in the summer wind. Lucinda, her daughter, reached for it, taking it gently between her finger and thumb.

"What is it?" Celia asked the three-year-old, bringing her camcorder to her eye and pressing the red Record button.

"Butterfly!" She held it up to her mother's camera.

Celia zoomed in, recording her young daughter's wide face, the soft, straight lines of her eyebrows beneath the center part of her brown hair pulled back in pigtails. The pointed chin dipped down beneath the sweet smile. And those cheeks. Celia could eat them up sometimes. "What color is it, Loochi?"

"Pink." Her dark eyes glowed beneath her wide, pale forehead. Celia had really never seen a cuter little girl. She was probably biased, but nevertheless, she thought she was right about that.

"No . . ."

Now, she may have been adorable, but as far as learning her colors . . .

Celia watched her daughter through the viewfinder as she held up the butterfly. Loochi's little face smiled beside the paper insect; her dark, glossy hair shimmered next to the fuzzy, opaque lightness of the butterfly's wings. She'd picked it out at the dollar store down the street.

"Green!" Lucinda cried.

"Good! Okay, now, what do butterflies do?"

"Fly!"

"Yay, that's great!" Sometimes Celia looked in awe at Lucinda, remembering how her sister and her friends told her she wouldn't realize how much a heart could love until she had children, that every biting pain, every moment of uncertainty was worth it.

"To the clouds?"

"To the clouds!"

Those women were right.

It was a special day, Celia decided right then. They'd play

for a little bit, take a walk, and order in a pizza. They never ordered pizza. Celia worked down at the shoe store. Even carryout was a luxury. It didn't matter, though. Lucinda loved frozen pizza almost as much. And Celia would let the butterfly watch *Beauty and the Beast* with them because she knew that's what Lucinda was going to ask. That crazy butterfly had lounged next to Lucinda on the arm of the couch for the past week.

Lucinda whirled and danced with the butterfly. Jumping up and down. A little jumping bean, skin glowing in the hot, summer sun. Celia kept the camera going. She just had a feeling she'd never want to forget this day.

Four

She hated this bathroom, the blue stucco walls, the old mirrored medicine cabinet, the sugar bucket she used as a trash can. When the toilet's a centerpiece, something's just wrong, and God bless the person who attached the scallop-shell lid on the thing. Nina needed reminders of the beach as often as possible.

Nina longed for her father just then, to see his wiry blond hair reflecting the sun, his green eyes hidden behind his cool Ray Bans, those ratty, khaki shorts he always wore in the summer. Gregory Daniels hadn't been the greatest father in the world. He blew his stack every once in a while when Nina came home too late or he smelled alcohol on her breath; he grounded her one night and took it back the next; he drank a little too much himself at times; he occasionally missed one of her dance recitals. But he knew how to laugh; he knew how to scoop her hands in his and do the shag, something he learned in his native South Carolina. They'd triple step and rock step on the wooden floor of the kitchen in time to "Under the Boardwalk."

Sometimes he took her to the beach, and there Nina's father would tell her about his views of life, what makes a person happy, why love usually comes as a big surprise.

"Why?" she asked him one day as they sat eating ice cream, great swirls of it on crunchy cones. She realized she probably remembered them twice as big as they actually had been. But that was her right. "Why is that?"

"Because most of us believe if someone knew the truth about us, they'd go running. Find someone who's not afraid of your truth, Nina. And when you do, by all means, don't marry him! That will ruin it."

"Really?"

He put his arm around her. "No. I'm kidding."

Nina stood by the old, square porcelain sink, the drain hole wreathed in rust, the spigot dripping at its usual three-second interval. She read the directions of the test kit, her nerves jumping and hopping, vibrating the paper. She memorized the instructions, then threw them, along with the box, into the sugar bucket. The instructions never came right out and said, "Pee on the stick," but they might as well have. That's what every woman always said when they talked shop. "Did you use the kind where you pee on the stick?"

So Nina peed on the stick. Hoping that just once, fate would be on her side.

Nina's life hadn't gone according to plan because the plan had been silly to begin with. That's what her mother told her the day she packed up the biggest suitcase she could find and moved into the city. Really, who honestly tried to make it as a dancer in New York? Not real people. Real people went to the clubs in the downtowns of their own cities, which in her case would have been Philadelphia, and people admired their steppiness and verve, and they danced there with pretty shoes, but shoe-store shoes nonetheless. They would have no idea how to execute a perfect paddle and roll or a riff-drop. And those people went back to the office or the schoolroom or the showroom the next day.

That's what real people did, what thinking, sensible people did.

And they were smart, Nina reasoned, looking at the second hand on her watch. Come on, who waited tables for four years in hopes of . . . what, Nina? She'd even stopped going to auditions two years ago, the voices of her mother and regular people who settled long ago for the hum-drum finally winning her over. The hum-drum knew the secret to life, right? They never put themselves out there and failed.

They knew better from the start. Besides, a person can only stand so much rejection, and so many of the directors and choreographers weren't even nice about it. A simple "no thank you" would have sufficed. Not the little morsels of cruelty some used to make themselves feel so smart and tony at the expense of other people's souls. Well, her soul maybe. Maybe some of the other dancers could forget the scathing put-downs, but those words festered inside of her still, telling her to just forget it. She didn't know why she gave all those voices such power, why she didn't learn to listen to her heart telling her to keep at it. But these days, at twenty-five, well, she felt old.

Now here she was, just bumbling along the concrete trails, letting life come at her, forgetting her keys, her pantyhose, forgetting the things her mother told her about boys before her father died and the advice stopped for good, forgetting that Manny, the owner of the restaurant where she worked, who treated his horses better than most of his wait staff, was ready to fire her if she was late one more time.

Okay, maybe she didn't forget that. Manny didn't let anybody forget anything.

The kitchen moved like some kind of geared device; several pairs of hands were chopping onions and garlic, seeding and peeling jalapenos, only to turn and dump them into bowls or pots. The dishwasher swiveled with trays of glasses and plates, setting them on the stainless steel drainboard.

José shook a saucepan of sweating onions, jarring the bits turning clear atop the heat of the large gas burner. Now, the smell of the early preparation was enough to bring anybody back to life, and he'd had a particularly rough night, begging for mercy to come in the form of sleep. Just a good night's sleep.

"Manny not coming in today?" Carlos asked as José brushed a mole sauce on a pan full of quail he'd spent most of the morning preparing. Carlos pointed to the expensive quail with the tip of his knife.

José flicked his brows upward. *"I'll take my chances."*

At least there'd been cooking to fall back on once the accident happened, something he learned to do as a little boy in Mexico. His mother and his grandmother each taught him their respective recipes for the same dishes; his father joined them sometimes as well. Cooking was life at the Suviran ranch, and after caring for the horses and the grounds, they could eat a table full of food. Even Manny knew how to make carnitas better than any of his relatives, roasting the pork to a golden brown, the meat so tender it fell apart between your teeth. Not that their father would admit that. But ah, well. Some familial arguments went on for generations and provided a familiar spark when they gathered. There was a pleasant beauty to it.

He lifted the heavy lid off the cast-iron pot of rice, the smell sticky and starchy and familiar. And how did he end up here? In this kitchen? There were times he was ready to pack a backpack, sling it over his shoulder, and just hit the road. Perhaps return to Mexico where his grandmother still lived with his aunt and uncle. Or maybe work odd jobs, moving along after a while, seeing places he'd never see otherwise. Never getting in a car, of course. He'd sworn off those years before. If a storm came, he'd find shelter in a nearby barn or gas station, and he'd wait until it blew over. That sort of timing made much more sense to him.

He didn't know why he didn't just take off. He stared into the enameled recess of the iron pot, the rice, the water, blurring as that day flashed before him again as it had been doing every day since he left himself behind, those memories. Shouldn't they have at least blurred at the edges by now? Loosened at their seams?

But still, he saw it all as clearly as the rice before him.

The shoes he wore that afternoon, pointed Italian shoes, sleek and elegant, typified what he was trying to become. A citizen of the world loved by all, wearing the best clothing, inhabiting the most fashionable places, becoming the man everyone else wanted to be.

Waiting to go to a press conference, he had danced with Jasmine outside the home of his manager, Francisco. Just a typical street in Brooklyn, brick row houses stacked together like library books, some stuccoed over, some covered completely in siding, some brightly colored in hues of red and yellow, others in white or tan. Iron fencing ran across some front yards, matching the railings flowing down beside the front stairs. Maple trees, leafed out in the sweltering summer day, grew from islands of soil in the cement sidewalks. Cars sat baking in the sun, the asphalt seemed ready to bubble, and José was already sweating through his clothes. Normally he was used to sweating, but today he'd hoped to remain cool.

Earlier he'd slicked back his hair and slid on the pressed pants and vest to his Armani suit, the one he'd bought on a shopping spree the day he signed the contract. He felt alive that day, his clean-shaven face open to the world, no hint of reticence as he twirled Jasmine to the beat of a song playing from a car some young men worked on nearby. He had everything he'd ever wanted and he knew it. Life was good.

"Now come back! Come back!" he said as he turned his manager's little sister, pulled her under his arm, and twirled her again. José loved to dance, to sway his hips and shoulders, to twist his ankles. At the clubs. In front of his mirror. With his mother. With his girlfriend.

The beautiful Caroline. Prettier even than Helen, who'd dated him as he rose to the professional level, Caroline planned to meet him that evening after the press conference.

Fine clothing and beautiful women would land him in magazines all over the world. Not a bad deal for kicking some leather around. Not a bad deal for a kid who spent his early mornings shoveling horse manure.

"Your brother would be late to his own funeral, Jasmine."

She blushed.

"Car!" The shout echoed off the parked cars and the faces of the houses.

José turned toward the boy who yelled, then picked up a soccer ball as he and the rest of the young players hurried to the sidewalk. The boy, ash brown hair cut close to his head, turned to one of his companions as he pointed to José. "I told you it was him!"

The others just nodded.

Eyes holding a few more years than his birthdays might suggest, he held out a ragged ball, so dirty and worn it was hard to differentiate the white hexagons from the black. "Would you?"

"What is this?" José popped the ball out of the boy's hands, bounced it once, then spun it around between his palms. "Nice ball. Wow. You guys play a lot, huh?"

They nodded. He pushed his thumbs into the ball, feeling the pressure. Good.

"Where do you play?"

The boy, obviously the group's spokesperson, jerked his head toward the road. "The street."

"The street? What about the cars?"

"We have to move every time. It stinks."

José reached out and mussed up the boy's hair. He knew if the game seethed in their blood, they'd play anywhere. He liked the way the boy looked at him, admiring but sizing him up all the same.

He leaned over to Jasmine and whispered, *"Go tell your brother to hurry up. We need to go."*

Back to the boys. "Okay! You, there!" He pointed from one boy to the other, positioning them along the sidewalk as he settled the ball on the ground. "You over there, you there, you here, and you here."

The boys snapped to. Most likely none of them figured when they came out to play that day that the most freshly signed player for Club Madrid would join them. Their lucky day, eh? José pointed to the only boy who'd said anything so far. "What's your name?"

The boy mumbled.

"Huh?"

"David."

"Are you ready, David?"

He nodded, mouth drawn in a grim line. José started forward, weaving through the boys where he had placed them. They turned and followed him.

José stopped and spun on his heel. They ground to a halt.

He held out his hands. "Where's the ball?"

The boys stared at his feet, confusion wrinkling their brows. They looked around back to where José began his run.

Oh. There it was. The ball. Almost stuck to the cement, it seemed.

José crossed his arms. "You guys are sleeping, huh?"

David hurried over, picked up the ball, and threw it to José.

José caught it. "Francisco!" he called back toward the house where he was staying. They were going to be late. He reached into his pocket for the Sharpie his manager slipped in there earlier for autographs, just in case. *"You never know, José,"* Francisco had said.

He signed the battered ball, and the boys grinned. "Hmm. My name looks pretty lonely on this ball. How about I get a few more names here for you? Like Tomas Cordoba."

"El Puma!" David cried.

"Uh-huh. But you'd better watch out. I might want to keep that ball for myself."

The boys looked from one to another, eyebrows raised, faces open. José had all the hope in the world for them. For himself too. But he needed to get going. How could one man take so long to get ready? "Francisco!" he yelled up to his manager again. "Francisco! *Come on, brother! Your little sister doesn't take this long."*

Finally.

Francisco jogged down the front steps. *"Don't hate me because I'm beautiful."* José could still remember his getup: black leather cap, a pink guayabera shirt, designer of course, loved by cigar smokers everywhere, only maybe not pink, but that was Francisco. An Argentine, Francisco spoke with his hands so much, José wanted to laugh. Well, since José himself wasn't allowed to use his hands, the privilege might as well go to Francisco.

Francisco clasped his watch around his wrist. *"Besides, Rome wasn't built in a day; this takes time."* He snapped his fingers. *"Let's go!"*

José held up the ball. "All right, guys. I'll bring this one back to you, I promise." They slapped hands, sealing the deal.

He threw the ball into the back of his convertible, feeling very sweaty and slightly heroic. "All right, let's go."

David crossed his arms. "What do we play with until you get back?"

José opened the car door. He turned to Jasmine, who was standing on the porch. "Ah, Jasmine. Can you get one of those practice balls Francisco keeps in his closet?"

She nodded and disappeared inside.

"No, no, no, José. Those balls are expensive."

José hit Francisco on the shoulder as he slid into the vehicle. Such a skinny guy. *"Relax! We're rich now."*

Francisco nodded. *"You're right."* He reached behind him to a cardboard box on the back seat, plucked a cap from inside, and handed it to David. "Call me if you ever need a manager."

Looking at himself in the rearview mirror, José licked his fingers and smoothed back his hair.

"Let's go, José," Francisco said, as if José had made them late.

Ah, well.

Jasmine threw a practice ball from Francisco's bedroom on the second story.

David ran toward it, leading the pack of boys.

"All right, I'm ready." José gripped the steering wheel.

Big day. Big, big day.

He slipped the key into the ignition of the car, a 1957 Bel Air. Long and black, shining chrome, restored leather interior. With Manny and his father's help, he'd spent hundreds of hours fixing it up. A different kind of car for a different kind of man. He'd show the world he was something else.

The engine breathed and hummed. José slipped it into drive, and the dual exhausts rumbled as he drove off down the simmering street with a friendly honk of his horn, he and Francisco raising number ones to the boys behind them. The sun warmed their shoulders and they felt like conquerors. Brooklyn today, Europe tomorrow. Who knew?

But they would drink it down to the dregs. José had promised himself that after all his family's hard work and sacrifice to get him to this point, he wasn't going to waste a second of it.

Francisco pulled out a leather cigar case from the glove compartment and chose two Cuban Cohibas. He undid the cellophane, snipped off the end of one with his cigar cutter, then handed it to José.

At the next stop sign, José popped it between his teeth and Francisco held his torch lighter up to the end. "You know not to inhale, right?"

José sat back, took a deep pull, and let the sweet flavor rush over his tongue. He blew out a thin, directed stream of smoke that the wind quickly disbursed and looked at Francisco like he was crazy.

Which he was. It was why he hired him as his manager. Francisco made everything a party. Or tried to. Today he had a tough job ahead of him, convincing José to charm the public at a press conference. José planned to make him earn his keep. Let Francisco sweat for a bit.

He took a right. *"I'm a soccer player, man. I hate interviews. I told you: I'm not a speaker."*

Francisco ran a hand over his buzzed, blond hair. *"Remember what to say, right? Let's practice."*

José grinned. *"In English or Spanish?"*

"English. Come on, José. Practice."

Talking to David and the gang was one thing, but this on-demand interview practice was another. José puffed on his cigar, trying to calm himself. Get him on the field and he didn't care what stood in his way. But interviews? He'd rather play one-on-eleven than sit with a microphone in his face. "I'm happy to . . . the opportunity . . . be here with all of you, with—"

"*Tell me. Where did you learn English? Hooked on Phonics?*" Francisco rolled his wrist, his own cigar circling its smoke. "*You have to say it with class. Maybe a little tear, a drop of emotion. 'I am thrilled to be here in this outstanding presence of you beautiful people.' Then you put on the hat.*" He took off his leather cap, placed the team hat on his head, and continued. "'I am . . . eh . . . ecstatic to be here in front of all you beautiful people today. I want to thank my wonderful manager, Francisco, et cetera, et cetera . . . Club Madrid, et cetera, et cetera.' *With great emotion. That's how you do it.*"

"Sí," said José with a grin. "*I've got an even better idea. You do the interview.*"

Francisco drummed his fingers on the door, replying in kind. "*You're right. I should do it. How do I look?*"

"*Like you were born for this.*"

Francisco winked. "*Seriously.*"

José jabbed his cigar toward the cap. "*That hat represents two million dollars.*"

"*Two point two. We don't round down.*"

José could feel the celebration winds that blew around his chest that day, remembering what Francisco said, the words still jabbing him as he worked in his brother's kitchen.

"*Tomorrow, José, you will be in every magazine from Canada to Argentina. Your face is going to be everywhere.*"

Yes, it would. But he needed to get through today, standing before reporters and photographers.

"*Are you sure we need to take these shortcuts through the neighborhood, Francisco? Can't we just get on 278?*"

"*You've come with me this far, brother. Trust me to get you where you need to go.*"

And José drove on. His sleek Italian shoes pressing the gas of his sleek old convertible. He sang with the music, cigar between his teeth. "'*Dance with me, make me sway . . .*' *Hey, where's the opener again? Is it Buenos Aires or Madrid?*"

"*Don't know yet. But I'm hoping it's in my homeland . . . I'm telling you, man, Argentinean women are gorgeous. Can't ask for more.*"

José loved this song. "'*. . . Only you have that magic technique, when you sway I go weak . . .*' *With their accents alone they get me.*"

"*Look, bro, they aren't perfect . . . but they are Argentinean.*" Francisco grinned, raising his eyebrows.

"*Yeah, too bad. Man, if you love it there so much, why don't you move there?*"

"*Same reason you don't move to Mexico.*" He ran his thumb along the tips of his fingers and lifted his eyebrows. It always came down to money.

José poked his cigar toward the sun. "*Do you know, bro, why Argentineans look up at the sky and smile whenever lightning strikes?*"

"*Why?*"

"*Because they think God likes them so much that he's taking pictures of them.*"

"*And you doubt that?*"

They drove along, music blaring, leaving the simple neighborhoods of Brooklyn in their wake.

Francisco pointed to José's shoes. "*Man, you can't be risking it in those shoes . . . playing on the sidewalk like that?*"

"*Don't worry about it.*"

Francisco turned toward him, his face earnest. "*I've heard that before. You get a injury and poof*"—he jerked a thumb toward his door—"*all those years in the minor leagues, everything you worked for, out the window.*"

The man worried too much. "*Look at you, the overprotective mama.*"

"*I'm serious. Something happens and who gets yelled at? They'll put you up in a luxurious rehab center with pretty nurses. But the suits will yell at the manager.*"

"*Okay, boss, no more playing soccer in the street. It's big business now.*"

Francisco sat back in his seat. *"You got that right. Your feet have a price tag."*

Six years later, there in that busy kitchen, José wanted to go back to that day. To that very moment. No, back to the shoe store when he bought those Ferragamos. That would be the moment because he had thought he deserved shoes like that, and when a man finds himself believing he deserves a pair of two-thousand-dollar shoes, he's already walked halfway down the road to trouble.

He never forgot the closing argument of the prosecutor who called him "a young man devoid of temperance, lacking the carefulness it takes to be a citizen in our society." And he had to agree with the man, even as he sat there with his lawyer, hoping and praying for a miracle. People got off for doing things far worse, his family kept saying. The sentence stunned them all to silence. They still rarely talked about it, and if they did, it was shrouded in terms like "the accident" or "when you were away."

He held up his hand and examined the palm, once smooth and white, now red, scarred, and calloused. He slid the rice pot off the gas burner and lowered his hand to the flame.

There. There.

Five

Manny shined his gold cuff links on his pants, then arose from his desk, ready to really begin the day. He'd finished the books, and now it was time to check on the kitchen. José usually did a great job, but some days he was so distracted.

How do you see your little brother go from clean-cut, outgoing soccer star to bearded, sober-faced cook without it hurting your heart just a little?

You don't.

It was just that simple.

But Manny knew that hard work and just pushing through solved most of life's ills. The best thing he could do for his brother was keep him on his toes, expect high and mighty things from him, and keep a watchful eye. The restaurant was good for José. Manny couldn't let him go back to being the shadow person he'd become in prison. Gaunt, haunted, inwardly playing the scene over and over again.

But José was good for the restaurant too. He had to admit that. The man could cook.

Manny had opened El Callejon eight years earlier on a small business loan, and he hadn't had a full night's sleep since. If he expected a lot from José and his staff, he expected even more from himself.

He ran a hand over the purple jockey silks hanging by the door, delivered the day before, then locked up his basement office and headed up the steps toward the main floor of his restaurant. He jokingly called El Callejon the love of his life when he first opened up. Now, well, the joke wasn't so funny. Thirty-six and married to the place, not to mention having just bought a thoroughbred, he had no time to find a wife. His mother was almost beside herself. *"No children from you. None from José. Only my baby gives me hope that someday, someday, Manny, I will be a grandmother."* She'd been praying for ten years now and so far, no grandchildren.

"Mama," he always told her, *"if you'd stop being so overcome with all of this, I think it would do you good."*

"I'm sorry, Manny. It's just that you and your brother would make good fathers."

If they were anything like Manny's father, that certainly would be the case.

"And now you buy this horse!" she had said just the other day. Of course his papa was thrilled that the family way of horses would continue here in America.

Manny stiff-armed the swinging door and stepped into the kitchen. Luscious yellow and green peppers, oranges, mangoes, and avocados awaited the knives of his cooks; flaming red peppers and tomatoes contrasted with the wooden cutting surfaces, the stainless steel, and the tile. Ever mindful of the Health Department and being of a meticulous nature himself, Manny demanded a clean kitchen. Everything was up to perfect standards. Everything, except his brother's huge beard. "Morning!"

Yes, all was moving along like a steam train. At the range, Pepito, a friendly faced young man wearing a black cook's cap, shook a large sauté pan of sweating onions. One of the other cooks—Manny couldn't remember his name—cut up a smoked pork loin and Manny pointed to it. "Make sure you get five cuts out of that." Let them get too generous and there would go his business. You had to keep an eye on every detail, every single one.

He headed over to the dishwasher and pulled a freshly washed piece of stemware from the tray. Good. Spotless. He'd gotten the dishwashing unit second hand when he opened and only luck and duct tape kept it from landing in the junkyard. He was certain of this because it surely was the only explanation.

Marco, a grizzled slightly double-chinned fellow with a close-shaved beard, seeded jalapeños at his workstation, throwing them into the blender.

"Marco, remember—not too many jalapeños. Too spicy, they won't eat it. They don't have the stomach we have."

He nodded at José, who looked glum and serious as usual, then Manny headed into the dining room, the aroma of cooking following him.

El Callejon had evolved over the years. He'd collected authentic Oaxacan art, fanciful carved animals in vibrant colors, and murals of everyday life that complemented the tan linens and grass green tablecloths.

The room buzzed with servers—men in loose white pants and shirts cinched together with crimson sashes, women wearing embroidered skirts and blouses, all polishing silverware or arranging tables or setting up the service alleys with extra glasses, plates, and cutlery.

Vases and vases of fresh, exotic flowers lent a carnival air to the place. Excitement. Celebration. That's what Manny wanted, as if to throw open the doors and tell the world, "Come. We Suvirans know how important life is, living is."

At least on his good days he knew. And today was going to be a good day. A very good day. He'd make sure of it.

His dining room manager, Pieter, stepped beside him. "Morning, Manny."

"Morning."

Manny never actually called Pieter by name, afraid to mispronounce it. According to the tax record, he reported him simply as "Peter."

Pieter took out his PalmPilot, ready to make notes. Manny thought he was a bit of a suck-up, but he did a good job, paid great attention to detail, and could find the most obscure ingredients imaginable.

They halted by the blond wood bar where Margarita, a waitress, folded linen napkins as she sat in front of the bar. Henry, the new bartender, a smiling sandy-headed Irishman with thick-lensed spectacles, polished stemware.

Manny pointed at him. "Henry, make sure to bring more than enough fresh mint to the bar."

Henry set down the glass. "You bet. I have the mojitos down."

"You better." Manny softened his words with a smile. "That's our signature drink."

As if Henry didn't know that. Sometimes he wondered at his own inability to let anything go. His mother told him he was ripe for a stroke. His youngest brother, Eduardo, called him a control freak.

Eduardo was too American these days. Especially with his new girlfriend. A model. What was her name again? Manny couldn't remember. But it sounded skinny, like she was. Manny preferred more robust women. A skinny girl gets sick, and imagine all the medical bills!

He pointed to Henry. "If they ask, say you're Irish-Cuban. I'm Mexican-Cuban. The whole place is something Cuban for the week."

He'd heard a convention of Cuban businesspeople was taking place at a hotel down the street. José was planning a special each day: boliche, costillitas, and lamb shanks. José had a way of cooking meat, rubbing it, massaging it with spices, that Manny himself couldn't replicate.

It was going to be a good week. He could feel it. They were ready.

He turned to Pieter and whispered, "Try Henry's new drinks and tell me how good he is."

Pieter made a note of that in his handheld, his stylus flicking in a quick step across the surface.

Manny approached the cheese table, the aroma of wedges of anejo, asadero, and Oaxacan cheese mixing with mangos, melon, and grapes. Manny dipped his pinkie in a bowl of dipping sauce. He brought it to his mouth, letting it touch the tip of his tongue. "That's a good sauce."

Yes, a very good day. And an even better weekend coming too.

Come Monday, the day they were closed, he'd drive out to the stables. Maybe he'd convince José to get out of the city with him.

He approached Amelia working at her tortilla station at the front of the restaurant. Amelia's fleshy arms vibrated with each push of her rolling pin, and she brushed aside a stray piece of hair that had escaped her bun. "Amelia!"

She smiled, baring her white, even teeth. Amelia always had a wide smile, and there was beauty in the wide forehead. She made him miss Mexico, her dark eyes sparkling almost as much as the jet earrings dangling from her earlobes. "Buenos días, señor."

Amelia worked hard. Manny appreciated dependable people.

A long table stretched down the middle of the dining room. "Nice. Very nice."

They knew how to do it right at his place.

Pieter looked around, tapping the stylus against his handheld. "Anybody seen Nina?"

Oh no. Manny looked at Pieter.

Rules were rules. Manny liked Nina, and she'd been here a long time, but lately . . . He headed back toward the kitchen. Maybe José would know something. The employees trusted him. Maybe it was those sad, doe eyes in which they found a quiet sympathy. Well, better José than himself. He had a business to run, and without that business, where would all these people be anyway, eh? Most of the other restaurateurs he knew weren't nearly so nice.

Six

Nina held the plastic stick up in the dim light trickling through the small, frosted bathroom window. The two blue lines might as well have been made of neon tubing, lit up and flashing, "Pregnant! Pregnant!" She threw it into the sink with a frustrated groan and kicked the trash can because, unlike Pieter, the sugar bucket was there. Why did the truth, showing itself in plain light, always feel worse than when it remained in the shadows?

But she knew. Now she knew.

She bumped her head against the mirror. Again and again.

No, no, no. This wasn't in her plans. Not in her grand plans. And not even in the "just-settling" plans.

Best just to get on with the day.

One more thing to do, though. She grabbed a phone book, looked up the second listing in the yellow pages.

Abortion Clinics.

Well, no use being cryptic about it.

Before it, Abortion Alternatives caught her eye. The first listing.

No.

There were no other options.

She dialed the number. A warm voice assured her everything would be okay, and it would be, wouldn't it? Women did this all the time and they survived.

"Yes, we had a cancellation for Wednesday. You're in luck," the voice said. "Is one-thirty all right?"

"Yes." Nina whispered the word, feeling another bout of nausea. She gave the woman her information. Was told what to not eat, how much the procedure would be.

"How will you be paying for this?" the woman asked.

Nina had no idea. Rent was due on Monday and her bank account was down to her last five hundred dollars. "Cash," she said, having no idea where she would get it, especially with rent due. "Yes. Cash."

She'd hope for the best.

A lot can happen between now and then, right?

She grabbed her wallet off the coffee table, shoved it in her purse, and left for work. There was no way she could take a shower, and she'd spent last night rolling around in bed, covered in the slick perspiration of dread. Well, knowing Manny, he'd overbooked the dining room and she'd be hoofing it anyway. No amount of deodorant could keep that kind of sweating at bay.

Pumping her feet along the cracked sidewalk, she called Pieter.

"I got the test results."

"Yeah?" He sounded hopeful.

"Positive."

"Oh."

"Yeah, so . . ."

"I was careful."

"Me too, Pieter."

Silence. "It's getting busy here, Nina. You should be at work."

She smashed the phone more tightly against her ear. "So, yeah. So I thought you'd want to know."

"Are you going to get it taken care of?"

"Me? Just me?"

"You know what I mean, Nina."

"I don't have that much money."

"I'll go halvsies with you on it," he said.

"Halvsies? Halvsies, Pieter? This isn't appetizers at Chili's."

"Man, Nina. This isn't easy for me either."

Oh brother. She could picture him with his slicked-back, faux European hair and attitude. Such a phony. Pieter. He'd grown up plain old Peter in Paramus, New Jersey. The rest of the staff thought he added the *i* to make himself seem French and up his chances of opening a restaurant of his own one day. "Look, I gotta go. We'll talk about the money after work, okay?"

"I'll write you a check for my half when you get here."

"You do that, Pieter. Sure."

"But you'd better hurry. Manny—"

She hung up, surprised at herself. She didn't think Pieter was the perfect guy, but she thought maybe he'd say something like, "Gee, Nina. I'm sorry. This must be so hard for you. I helped get you into this mess. I'll help you whatever way you think you need to go here." Nope. Nothing like that.

And I'm having his child. Oh man.

She felt like the idiot of the century.

How come this never happened to the *Sex in the City* girls? They did a lot more than she ever did.

Manny entered the kitchen, walking right up to José's station where he stood chopping peppers. José knew that look on his brother's face. So the day's troubles were already beginning.

"José, what's up with Nina? She was late yesterday, and today she is forty-five minutes late. That's two days in a row, plus calling in sick last week at the last minute makes three, and you know what happens at three."

Everybody knew what happened at three. José swore Manny would fire himself if he was late three times. "She'll be here."

Manny looked around the busy kitchen and said softly, "I can't run my business like this. I just can't."

Carlos, a Cuban with eyebrows like caterpillars and an open gaze, held out a saucepan toward José. "Try this, José."

José dipped the tip of his knife into the sauce. Not bad. Better than the cook's last try. "A little more epazote."

Manny snapped his fingers, and the cook turned the pan toward him. He dipped in a finger and brought it to his mouth. José studied his face. He wanted to disagree, José could tell, but he shook his head and grinned.

"Just a little bit," Manny said with a laugh.

Yes, there was the brother who had first played soccer with him. José shook his head. Manny.

"What's for family dinner?" Manny glanced at his watch. "It's almost ready, yes?"

"Yeah. Chiles rellenos and roasted quail in mole rojo."

"What?" Manny leaned down to examine the pan of

quail through the shelves of José's workstation. "That's a pretty fancy family dinner."

"The chiles are going bad, man."

Manny tapped his fingers on the stainless-steel surface of the workstation window. "I'm talking about the quail, José. It could have been a special." He stood up straight. "Oh, I see how it works. You just make the fancy staff orders and I pay for them, right?" He leaned forward. "Wrong. We cook for the customers, not for the staff. Next time you feed them *tacos and rice. Period!*"

José nodded like he'd hop to and obey those orders in the future. But he wouldn't. He made the quail on purpose. If Manny wasn't going to pay some of these people in the kitchen, illegals mostly, a fair hourly wage, he'd pay in food. It was only right.

Nina thought about calling her mother. No. Not now. She wished she could call her father. He'd have been there for her. She smiled when she imagined the conversation they'd have had. She always pictured him sitting on the beach.

"Dad, I'm pregnant."

"Oh, so the virgin birth is happening again, is it?"

She'd smile, just a little sideways grin. "It's Pieter's."

"Never did like the guy."

Or he wouldn't have, had he met him. To her father, all people were fashioned of cellophane.

"Come back home. Your room's the same. I'll take care of you."

And then the truth of it would have hit him.

"Doggonnit, Nina! I raised you better than this!" And he would have remembered the fact that he was going to have to face his family, and they'd be judgmental because Gregory was the one who never quite lived up to his potential, and wasn't this proof? Didn't it just figure? Well, the apple didn't fall far from the tree, they'd say, because her father's family wasn't exactly original in the speech department.

She'd make excuses to her dad, right there on the cell phone, about how she needed to get to work, how she was almost there, which she was, how she was sorry. But she lived in a big city, millions of lonely people, and besides, she was twenty-five, Dad, and how many twenty-five-year-old females were still celibate?

She'd work her shift and he'd leave five voice mails, the first one a little clipped, the final one saying how sorry he was for getting so upset and call him back. Please.

That's how it would have shaken down if he'd lived into the age of cell phones. But he hadn't.

He would have told her what she could say to soften Manny's heart when she walked in late, but what on earth could she possibly say to "three strikes you're out" Manny that would convince him to let her keep her job?

Not one person Manny ever fired had come up with the lucky phrase. And today, well, she wasn't one of the luckiest people in the world to begin with.

Seven

Okay, Loochi. Ready to play again?"

"Yes!"

Celia hated hide-and-seek, and it figured it was Loochi's favorite game. Her sister warned her about that sort of thing too. "Okay, I'm going to count . . ."

She hid her eyes. "Ten . . ."

Something inside of her always stuttered when Lucinda ran from her view. *Don't go!* she always thought, for sometimes two people are all each other has, and this was very much the case with Celia and her daughter.

"Nine . . ."

Her husband was killed overseas even before the baby was born, and Celia had almost lost Lucinda at birth.

"Eight . . ."

But Celia kept her alive by sheer force of will, demanding the doctors, the nurses, God, even that still little baby, blue, not breathing, to live. Live!

"Seven . . ."

And so Lucinda did live, sucking in a breath, finally, at the raging shout of her mother who, by all that was right, wouldn't let this child go without a fight. "Breathe!" she had screamed, the word ending in a pitch that caused one of the nurses to hold her hands against her ears.

"Six, five, four, three, two . . . one! Ready or not, here I come!"

Celia opened her eyes.

"Cheese!" Lucinda, still right in front of Celia, held out the butterfly.

"Sweetie, this is the part where you're supposed to hide."

"I see you!"

Celia laughed. "I see you too. We're going to play this game a lot when we go to Grandma's. She has horses and pigs and cows."

"Moo!" Lucinda scrunched up her smooth brow.

"Moo! That's right!"

Celia just couldn't bring herself to leave the apartment she and Scott moved into five years before.

"Play again!"

Lucinda scrambled off and Celia covered her eyes, counting backward from ten. Again.

"Ready or not, here I come!" She opened her eyes and saw no trace of Lucinda. Maybe the three-year-old was finally getting the hang of the game.

"Loochi?" She peered beneath the back porch and all around the small garden behind their first-floor apartment, where they'd planted bulbs the previous autumn. Now irises bloomed and the daylilies were broadcasting a sunny tint against the greenery. The crocuses were long gone, most of them ending up pinned in Lucinda's hair, and when Lucinda made enough of a fuss about it, in Celia's as well. One morning they walked to the store with at least ten blossoms each in their hair. Lucinda told her they looked like flower queens.

"Loochi, where are you?"

No. Not behind the snowball bushes either.

"I'm coming!" she yelled.

Not in the yard at all, as a matter-of-fact.

Fear trilled down the back of Celia's neck to the base of her spine. "Loochi?!"

Eight

José wished Pepito would turn off that radio, but instead the cook turned up the volume of the sports show. "The Mexican National soccer team will face the United States in New Jersey in the Gold Cup elimination game."

So. The Mexican National team would be in the area soon. José hoped his old manager, Francisco, would not be traveling with them. Francisco managed several players now and was doing quite well for himself. This came as no surprise to José.

He poured chopped green tomatillos in the blender and set it to whirring, his former hopes of coming face-to-face with that very team welling in his chest cavity. Knowing Manny, he'd somehow get them in the restaurant because it was "good for business."

José threw some wilted greens in the sink, then flipped on the garbage disposal. The water swirled in the suction, a whirlpool of greenery, leaves, and stems that joined together. He stood, mesmerized, immune to the game on the radio and the squeal of the blender, sweat pricking his brow. What looked like a butterfly, green and papery, swirled down the drain.

That day. That day. His hand smarted from the earlier burn, but instead of bandaging it like he usually did, covering up the blistered, angry flesh, he gripped the edge of the sink, becoming not so much oblivious to the pain as wrapped up inside the exquisiteness of the sensation. You are still alive, it told him.

Manny stepped into the kitchen and saw his brother over the sink. Two years had passed since José had been released from prison. In that time he'd come further than Manny would have thought possible. For six months José had stayed in an apartment their parents set up for him, reading books, eating the simplest of foods. Few of his old friends from his soccer days remained, and the ones who showed up usually stood at the apartment door, knocking and knocking and knocking.

They'd give up after several minutes, and after a while they gave up completely, telling Manny they tried.

Manny and his parents talked about it, their words flying back and forth across the kitchen table on a Sunday morning in January. *"He can't live like this anymore, Mama,"* Manny said. *"You have to do something."*

His mother nodded, her black hair, parted in the middle and gathered in a bun, picking up the overhead light. Blue lights streamed along the strands. *"I grieve for him. He is gone."*

"He cannot forgive himself," his father said, his brown eyes turned down at the corners, his mustache doing the same.

So much sadness.

Mama grabbed Manny's forearm that morning. *"Hire him at El Callejon."*

"What? No, Mama. I'm still trying to get this restaur—"

"Please, Manny. You've been in business for six years. Manny. Please."

Manny turned to his father, who shrugged. No help there.

"You know he can cook!" she said. *"He's even better than you were."*

"Now, now—"

She took his hand, kissed it. *"Please, my son. Just for a little while and then, if it doesn't work out, we can find something else. He can come back here and stay with us until he heals."*

"He may never heal," Papa said.

"No! Do not say that." Mama's eyes flashed like drops of oil on a rainy street. *"He will."*

And now, in the kitchen, Manny leaned toward his brother. José still zoned out much too often. And the burns. His family hadn't figured out what José was doing to himself. But Manny knew. He kept it to himself, however. It obviously met a need his brother had or he wouldn't show up occasionally with his hand bandaged. It didn't seem to affect his work, and he kept quiet about it.

"You ready, right?" he asked José.

José nodded and looked back down in the sink. He was holding back tears. Manny could read his brother's face like he read his wristwatch, which told him it was almost time to unlock the front doors.

José came to life. "Let's go! Marco! Andale, andale, jefe!"

He'd give Mama and Papa a call later, warn them José might be slipping back. But right then he had a restaurant to run, and he was going to make sure it ran like Secretariat at the Preakness. First, family dinner. He liked to think of his staff as family. But he wondered what role he played. Grouchy uncle?

Several minutes later, the staff gathered alongside the long table spread like a runner down the center of the restaurant. They began passing bowls of beans and rice and the chiles rellenos.

Manny stood at the head of the table, a list of specials in his hands. "Shrimp and crab legs over Mexican sweet black rice. Squash with a papaya lemon oil." Cutlery began to clink against the white bone china. "There are three boxes of shrimp in the walk-in, people, so push it, push it, push it!" He snapped his fingers. "By the end of the day, this item should be eighty-sixed in my kitchen. The last special is scallops. I think you've all served this before, so I'm not gonna say anything else about it."

José entered the room, holding the quail, hand bandaged now. Good. Surely the Health Department wouldn't appreciate it if they came in and saw his chef with a hand like that. That is, of course, if they could get past the beard.

Time to share the good news.

"I've got a special treat, Pepito. This coming Friday the Mexican National Soccer Team, along with the coach, will be here for the Gold Cup. They play the United States out in Jersey next week. I'm putting them in Kevin's section."

Manny looked at each person as they ate his expensive quail. He sighed. Well, there was nothing to be done.

"Also, there will be no autographs. If you want one, you can ask me, and I will ask them personally."

And where was Nina, eh?

He leaned down. "Get a sub for Nina, and, Pieter, gather up her things from her locker."

Pieter hesitated. "Do you think—"

"Don't question me. Just do it."

Pepito reached for the rice. "I'm starving."

Amelia smiled. "You're always starving."

"I'm starving when El Callao cooks. You got that right."

Henry, the new bartender, reached for the water pitcher. "El Callao? Why do you guys call him that?"

"Means 'quiet one' in Spanish. It's easier to pull a tooth than to pull a word out of him," Carlos said.

Amelia patted José's hand. Manny noted the tenderness in her eyes. She'd never looked at him that way. "He speaks to me all the time."

Nina approached the door of Manny's midtown restaurant. An hour late, she thought up all sorts of excuses. Water main break that flooded her apartment. A shooting on the way to her subway station. Emergency phone call from home.

Oh, that's right. Her mother wouldn't call her if her life depended on it. Nina thought of the last conversation they'd had five years before. Mother talked about the latest season of her favorite sitcom and wouldn't it be nice if everybody had good friends like that silly group, how she needed a new roof but just couldn't bring herself to get quotes, even about the stray cat, the sweetest little gray fur ball imaginable, coming around. After she'd asked Nina how she was doing, she'd interrupted her answer. "Oh, and did you see that new cop show on that cable channel?"

Nina had hung up the phone and realized that during the eighteen months since she'd left for the city to dance professionally, her mother hadn't called her once. So Nina made herself a cup of tea and asked herself if she should torture herself any longer by trying to maintain a relationship, putting in 100 percent when she shouldn't be carrying the primary burden in the first place.

So Nina experimented. She waited for a month. No call from Mother. Then Nina called. The conversation could have been the same with the replacement of different shows and an update on the cat and the leaking roof.

Next time she waited two months.

Then four, then a year. And now she had to admit even a TV-watching, roof-procrastinating mother would be better than nobody. Maybe the news that Nina was pregnant would bring her out of TV land.

Surely Mother would say something about a *grandchild*.

Nina pulled on the door handle. Her arm jerked. Locked. Okay, other door. The restaurant wasn't officially open yet. She walked a few steps, pulled on that door. Locked as well.

Nina shielded her eyes and peered in the large front window of the restaurant. She knocked on the plate glass, leaned forward as far as she could. And there they sat at the table, eating family dinner, the entire staff, staring at her, forks or water glasses suspended. Pieter stood up, then froze as Manny turned and made for the entrance.

She rushed toward him as he unlocked the door, then blew out onto the sidewalk.

"Manny, I'm sorry."

He silenced her with an upheld hand. "I don't want to hear it."

"Look, I had things—"

"Things?" Nostrils flaring, he pointed inside at the staff gathered for dinner. "You see Amelia? Three kids, Nina. She comes down here from the Bronx every day. Want to know how many days she's been late in the last eight years?" He joined thumb and forefinger together to form an *O*. "Zero, Nina. Zero."

"I know. I know how hard that must be."

"You know? You know? You know?"

He looked like he was ready to bite her. This was even worse than she'd imagined. Four years she'd worked for him, and she didn't like him any more than she did the first week when he railed her out for not filling up people's water glasses quickly enough. And you'd think she hadn't learned anything in all that time, the way he hovered over her, nitpicking, always finding fault.

"Manny, I didn't mean—"

"Okay, so then *you know* how easy it would be for you to find another job."

He straightened up, looked around him, and turned away, heading back toward the door. Pieter stood in the doorway. He whispered something to him.

José stepped outside.

Panic whittled at Nina's pride. Not today! She needed that money. "Manny, please! Give me another chance! I promise I'll make everything good." It was Friday, and tonight there'd be big tips, maybe enough for Wednesday's appointment. "How could you be so . . ."

No. Let it go, Nina. You're sounding like a grade-schooler.

Manny stopped, turned, and walked toward her, each step punctuating his diatribe. "So . . . so what? Unfair? It would be unfair, in fact, if I *didn't* fire you. It would be unfair to your coworkers for me to let them continue doing *your job*." He stopped, finger in her face. "This is the second day in a row, Nina. Not counting the times people looked the other way or—or covered for you."

"What are you talking about?"

"You called in sick twice last week, then you show up to work hungover."

Hungover? What in the world? "No. I was not hungover."

"It's too much, already."

"Manny, I was *not* hungover. I was sick!"

José rarely meddled in Manny's business, but Nina had been one of their most dependable waitresses. If he couldn't see something was happening with Nina, he wasn't looking closely enough.

Manny spun around, eyes hard. "Seeing how the other half lives, José? Stay out of this!"

José didn't want trouble. He just didn't want this to escalate. If Manny was going to fire Nina, fine. But this berating while the staff looked on: too much. Just too much. Even for Manny.

Manny pushed past his brother, back into the restaurant.

Pieter scurried out the door, arms overflowing with Nina's belongings: a pair of sneakers, a T-shirt, a makeup case, a paperback, and a stuffed bear. José liked Pieter even less than Nina liked Manny. The little suck-up.

Nina took the box. "Oh, thank you. Thanks, Pieter. That's nice." She turned and headed back down the sidewalk toward the subway station. Fired.

José pushed past Pieter and hurried behind her. At the end of the block, she tucked her belongings under her arm, not noticing as the small stuffed bear tumbled to the ground.

José hesitated. Should he? This wasn't exactly step ten in the hermit's handbook. The bear almost got stomped on by a woman in high-top sneakers. That settled it.

He hurried forward. He'd always liked Nina, occasionally standing with her out back on her smoke breaks when he needed a break as well. She didn't speak about much more than the latest book she'd been reading or movie she'd rented, but he liked the sound of her voice and that she knew little about him other than the fact that he was the owner's brother and was nicknamed "The Quiet One" by the rest of the staff. Nina wasn't a gossip. He liked that about her too. She smiled a lot, but he knew a lonely soul. José saw people like him and Nina on the street all the time, pain stitching them all together with its scarlet thread, arm to arm, hip to hip.

He hesitated, scooped up the bear, and rushed forward. "Nina!"

"Nina!"

Nina thought she was being followed. She whirled around, people snaking past her as they hurried to get through the turnstile and down to the tracks.

Oh. Just José. Good.

José stopped, her bear in his hand. She didn't realize she'd dropped him. If she'd gotten home and that bear was gone, well, that would have just been the final, screaming exclamation point to the worst day of her life since her father died.

And Pieter! She never thought he was filled to the brim with courage and integrity, but that was ridiculous. Yes, they'd kept what happened a secret from the rest of the staff, neither Nina nor Pieter wanting them to jump to the wrong conclusion. But couldn't he have at least refused to get her things? Even for the principle of the thing? She didn't get pregnant on her own.

José's dark blue eyes softened as he held out the bear. "He's unconscious, but I think he'll survive."

She'd never heard him string that many words together at once.

Oh, this little bear. John Bubbles. She'd named him after her favorite tap dancer when she received him on her twelfth birthday. They'd been through so much together. "Thank you." She smiled and held up the bear, jiggling him a little. "I guess I'll see you around."

She started toward the turnstile.

"Hey, why were you late? You know my brother."

Nina stopped. "Oh, trust me. I know your brother. He's a jerk."

A woman dressed for the office pulled up behind her. "Excuse me. Are you going in?"

Nina's nerves were stretched so tightly, she wanted to scream, but she moved aside. "Go ahead. Sorry."

"Thank you."

"He didn't have to humiliate me like that in front of everyone, José. I've been working for him for four years!"

She took advantage of a break in the flow, swiped her

card, and pushed her way past the barrier. José was nice and she knew he meant well, but really, "rules are rules" didn't make what Manny did any easier. At least he didn't use the "this is no way to run a restaurant" line on her that Manny always did. She hated that. She looked up at José, the man of secret sorrows, kindness accompanying the pain in his eyes. How could two brothers be so different? "And you tell him that I wasn't hungover. I was really sick!"

Starting for the train, she hesitated. José deserved better than that. And Manny should know what he really did back there. She turned back, grabbed the tubing of the bars that separated her from scruffy José. "I'm pregnant."

His face froze.

She grated out a laugh. "Yeah. This is one of the first mornings I haven't thrown up."

José looked down. The Quiet One.

She waited, and when no words came—"Okay. I've had enough for today." She held up Bubbles again. "Thank you. You'd better get back to your boss man."

Why was she taking this out on him?

Just get home, Nina. Make a cup of tea, slip in a DVD of Fred Astaire, and try to make it through until Wednesday.

José knew he couldn't let her go. Something inside him pricked his brain and he shouted, "Wait! Wait, Nina!"

She turned back.

"So what now?" he asked.

Her lips turned down. "Guess I have to figure that out, right?"

"You want to talk about it?"

She paused as if she were considering whether or not to pick up the earth and place it on her shoulders. She passed the Metro Pass to him through the bars. "They don't need a waitress; why would they need a chef?"

Good. Good, good, good. He had no idea where she was going, but he had all day to be gone from the restaurant. At least until the lunch rush was over. If he was going to anger Manny, he might as well go all out. The result would be the same either way.

José took the card, swiped it, and joined her.

The prep work was finished. All Manny had to do was find somebody to run the line. Simple.

Manny figured he just needed to cool off. He fell back into his leather desk chair and massaged his temples with the thumb and middle finger of his left hand. Staring at the jockey silks, he began to calculate how many years it would be before he could hire somebody else to run this place while he threw himself full time into racing. Not soon enough, apparently, judging by the headache knocking on his brain.

Pieter's shadow fell across his desk, his face stretched with panic. "José left."

"What do you mean 'left'?" He jumped from his desk, tore up the stairs and back out onto the sidewalk. Nothing there but the construction crew marring the late morning with the jarring sounds of their equipment. Despite that, Fifth Avenue never seemed so deserted.

"Who's going to run the line?" Pieter asked.

"José is gonna run the line."

That was that. He'd come back. José had no life, no place to go, nothing really to do with himself. He'd closed himself in. He'd be back. Besides that, he had to be. Because when it came down to it, José knew how to run that line better than anyone at El Callejon. There was no getting around it.

"What's the matter with you? You sick?" Manny asked.

Pieter shook his head. "No."

"Because I need you, man. You can't bug out on me like Nina. And what's the matter with that girl anyway? You know?"

Pieter shook his head again and made for the door.

"Everybody's flaking out on me today," he mumbled, reaching for a roll of antacids in his jacket pocket.

Nine

Nina and José sat on the subway train, the sickening fluorescent lights turning everybody's skin a shade yellower than was normal. Light yellow. Yellow ochre. Golden brown. The car was packed, some unfortunate people hanging on to the overhead bars. Nina fixed her eyes on a particularly dark man with baby dreads and full-grown bling, a large gold cross hanging from a thick chain around his neck. His high cheekbones as well as his dark glasses reflected the lights. She suspected he might be asleep behind those glasses. Lucky guy. Because here she sat with José, who was trying to be supportive but couldn't seem to say a word. Any conversation Nina ever had with José had been superficial. Friendly, yes, warm, somewhat, but never anything of internal importance to either of them. How could it be? She basically talked and asked him yes-or-no questions.

Why are you here? she wanted to ask him. She wanted to turn to him and say she didn't know what was driving his sudden need to befriend her, but . . . but what would she say after that? I'm glad you're here? I'm lonely and have nobody else, really? Gee, you know underneath that big beard you're pretty cute? And hey, as long as we're talking, why the beard in the first place?

She rolled her eyes, berating herself for being stuck in this situation. And there sat a pregnant woman three seats away rubbing her protruding belly. Just what she needed to see. A little girl, probably four years old with a dozen twisted ponytails and a gold hoop in each ear, stared at her, huge brown eyes stuck in her perfect brown skin like buttons on a pillow. She lifted her angel lips in half a smile.

Nina looked away.

None of that. Cute little people were what babies turned into. And babies, well, she didn't want to think about babies right now.

Four teenagers pulled out some five-gallon buckets, a shaker, and some cans. "Excuse me, ladies and gentlemen!" said what appeared to be the youngest of the group, his hair in cornrows, his smile, too many gold teeth notwithstanding, that of a born showman. "We are the Drumatics, and we would like to entertain you. After our presentation, donations will gladly be accepted."

The rhythm began, the hollow *thunk* of the buckets and the echoing metallic thrumming of the cans, the scratch of the shakers—back and forth, back and forth.

Oh man, Nina thought. It was one thing when performers did their thing in the stations. You could turn your back. You could walk away. You could turn up your MP3 player. But now they were stuck between here and there, at the mercy of all this noise.

The teen moved and clapped along with the percussionists, his open smile inviting people to join him in enjoying such amazing feats of rhythm—or something. A couple of tourists clapped. The rest, jaded New Yorkers like Nina, hunkered down into their magazines and newspapers. They didn't ask for this.

Nina held Bubbles, squeezing the little bear more and more tightly as the drumming increased in intensity. She looked down at her hands, trying to think about something else, trying not to feel so awkward next to José, who quite honestly looked like *he* wasn't actually sitting in the train, as if he'd hired some stand-in to sit there and let the everyday things of this world roll off his back.

"Give it! Give it!"

What now?

She twisted Bubbles's arm.

Two seats down and across the aisle a woman sat with her grandson who stood with his feet planted firmly apart, screaming and yanking on the plastic sword she held at the hilt.

"Give it to me!"

Little brat.

"No, sweetie. It's too dangerous on the subway. You could hurt someone."

The Drumatics, in an attempt to drown out the boy, turned up the volume even further.

"Give it! Give it!"

Pull and yank and scream and yell.

"No!" the grandmother, not to be outdone, hollered back.

The hands of the drummers moved faster and faster, the *thunks* and *pops* slamming into Nina's head.

She twisted Bubbles in her hands. Harder and harder.

This was turning out to be the longest subway ride she'd ever experienced. And while she knew the drummers were only trying to make a buck or two, she'd have appreciated a little quiet about now.

Oh, that's right. The little boy was still yelling anyway, his shrill screams and jutting lip calling attention to just how wonderful child raising can be. Right?

Right?

The brakes squealed as the train pulled into the station.

What was she going to do with José? Invite him back to her apartment? What would they say to each other? She felt fresh out of good ideas.

Guess I'm a little preoccupied.

She knew he had a secret. But Manny stayed mum, and if any of the staff knew what had dragged José into the realm of the walking wounded, none were letting on. Not that they didn't hypothesize: unrequited love, a crime on which he was waiting out the statute of limitations, some even thought he might be a burnout. Nina didn't. He wasn't that far gone. *Tortured* and *gone* were two different things.

Anytime a new waitress came, she ended up with a crush on José that lasted about a week until she realized there was no hope in starting up something with him. Even Nina had felt a pleasant little tumble of the stomach when Manny first brought him in, but, well, there was too much baggage there, obviously, and she definitely did not need more of that, no matter how nice-looking the luggage was.

The little girl, eyes wide, pointed to the bear and said, "Look."

Bubbles's arm was torn almost complete off his body.

Nina glanced up at the girl, forced the tears back behind her eyes, and shoved the little bear into her backpack. "I'm sorry," she whispered and stood to her feet.

José followed her off the train.

Manny had taken off his jacket half an hour before. Sweat ran down his face. He rolled up his sleeves and wiped the perspiration away with his forearm. This was not good. Not good at all.

This was not a good day.

He spooned some sauce over the fish entrée he was plating. "It's all about the presentation," he said to Pepito. "We don't need him. We don't need him." If he said it with enough confidence, maybe they'd believe him. Maybe he'd believe himself.

José, José, José!

Pieter, as rushed as everybody else, hurried into the kitchen, picked up a knife, and began chopping green chiles. "Maybe your mother and father will know where to find him."

Manny glanced sideways at his dining room manager. Truth was, Pieter, who'd never liked José, was always trying to undermine José's popularity with the kitchen staff and never made a dent. He had a cousin in Buffalo dying to move to New York, and Pieter wanted Manny to hire him as the chef. So Pieter always cast José in a bad light to Manny, but Manny saw through it. He kept Pieter on because Pieter knew where to find the freshest ingredients and had enough connections to negotiate the best prices delivered in the shortest amount of time. Not only that—

Pieter was easy to boss around. Let him try his maneuverings; Manny would keep José on because José was his family and somehow they'd make things work.

He handed Marco the spoon. "Take over. I've got to make a call."

Marco stepped on the line. "You got it."

So Manny called and complained to his mother, getting her upset, trying not to make it seem like he was making her feel guilty for asking him to hire José in the first place, which was exactly what he was doing. And there she sat in her cozy house near the beach worrying.

Truth was, he would have called her eventually, but now he had Pieter to blame. Well, good. He paid Pieter well enough for that.

The line was quickly falling apart, food arrangements falling over as they sat on the window, runny sauces bleeding over from entrée into side dish. The beans had scorched in one of the first pots Manny had ever bought for the restaurant.

Yes, he had a sentimental side.

He could see José's raised brow. Sentimental? Or cheap?

He wanted to prove to the staff and to José that he could run this line just as well as anybody. But finally, enough was enough.

He picked up the glaring red phone on the wall, the

one with buttons the size of tea bags, and punched in his brother's mobile number. Ringing began on the other end. Manny held up a hand as the ringing began. "Shh!"

He cocked his head to the left, listening. The ringing . . . was in the room?

There sat José's mobile phone near his usual post.

Manny picked it up, saw his own number flashing in the display, then slammed it down on the counter.

Ten

Nina pulled out a ten and handed it to a clearly relieved Carla. "Thank you so much."

"No problem." Carla eyed José with suspicion. Nina wanted to laugh. If this baby was José's, she wouldn't be in the same pickle. José would take care of his responsibilities by doing something more than suggesting "halvsies," that was for sure.

Pregnancy kit paid for. Good.

She turned to José. "Want to go to the park?" That was a lot better than her apartment.

"Okay."

They stepped out into the sunlight, walked in yet more silence to the park bench. They sat down as a group of Haitian nannies, their charges in strollers, crossed the sidewalk in front of them. This mystified Nina. "I thought the point of having children was to raise them. You know the parents make enough money to support three families. They should stroll their own babies."

It was bad enough her father was not around because he had died. *Imagine*, she thought, *never having your parents around and they weren't dead?* Yeah, that would make a kid feel really special. All the nice clothes, good schools, and positive messages on PBS kids' shows couldn't counteract all that. Well, her kid, when she had one someday, wouldn't have to worry about never seeing her. She wouldn't be that kind of mom.

You're already a mom.

Oh, shut up, she thought.

José stood up and slipped a hand in the front pocket of his jeans. He dug out . . . nothing. He began patting all of his pockets. "I have to call my brother."

"You don't have your cell phone?"

"I must have left it in the kitchen."

She reached into her backpack and pulled out her own. She jerked a thumb toward a nearby bodega. "Here. I'm going to get a soda."

Manny's head snapped up as the red phone on the kitchen wall started to ring. He laid down his knife, blade resting on a pile of mangled red onions. His eyes protested and he blinked away the tears. "Pepito! Chop these onions."

"Sure, boss." He didn't look too happy about it.

He brushed his hands on his apron, picked up the receiver, and cleared his throat, trying his best to sound calm and professional. "El Callejon, how may I help you?"

"Manny?"

"José? Where are you?"

"I'm with Nina."

Just as he'd figured. "Who the heck is Nina? I'm your brother. I fire people all the time, José, and you don't go running around after them."

"I know, man, I know."

Servers bustled around him. Runners grabbed plates and still they did not get them from the window fast enough. Some returned with meals that had gone cold. It was a good thing he didn't have his ego tied up in his cooking. But still, his restaurant was suffering. And that meant more to him than anything.

Pretty sad. And he thought José had no life?

The thought angered him. "When are you coming back?"

"I need to help Nina right now."

"You need to do what? You need to be here. In this kitchen. Cooking. Doing *your job*. Come back right now."

"I can't. I can't."

"What do you—what do you mean you can't?"

"Some things are more important than cooking, Manny."

Manny gripped the phone, storming away from the wall to grab a twist tie off one of the plates on the tray Margarita was hefting out to the dining room. "Listen to me, idiota! If you're not here in the next ten minutes, you'd better be at the unemployment office."

He looked down in his hand and grated out his frustration. He'd pulled the phone cord out of the wall. Beautiful. Just beautiful.

Margarita hurried off as Manny slam-dunked the receiver into the trash can.

José sat in front of the store, waiting for Nina to emerge. This was the first time he'd gone out on a limb in years, and now this? For Nina? A woman he barely knew?

The thing was, Manny *would* fire him. And all in the name of what was best for José. He could picture the conversation.

"José, I hate to do this, but I'm your brother and I want what's best for you. Sacrificing my business wouldn't do either of us any good."

A man slammed out of the door of the bodega, cursing, a few bills crumpled in a meaty fist set below a forearm covered in a dragon tattoo. José shrugged. Angry people. New York. Nothing new.

He looked around him at the same weary streets and

crumbling curves and realized he was ready for a change in life. That was for sure. Every day the same. Keeping anything with a pulse at arm's length.

He unwound the bandages on his hand, wincing as the gauze stuck in the crevices of his wounded palm. The flesh was flaring in an angry red, blistered and seeping.

This isn't penance.

He widened his eyes, his own thoughts surprising him.

That was right. It wasn't penance at all. It created a way he could fool himself into thinking he was such a horrible person he could hide from the world and be justified.

He wrapped it back up.

A suited businessman wearing fine shoes pushed a dollar bill into an empty paper coffee cup by José's feet and walked into the store.

José plucked it out and shoved it in his pocket. Oh well. Maybe today was his lucky day.

Nina exited the bodega and he stood up.

"Oh man, that was crazy," she said.

"What happened?"

"Did you see that guy rush out?"

José nodded. "Very angry."

"He had a run-in with the cashier. It sounded like the clerk, who was Chinese, was speaking Spanish. Just a typical New York moment." She looked around her. "I'd hate to have to leave this place."

They walked by a parking lot, a high chain-link fence lining their path to the right.

"Why would you leave?"

"It takes money to live here, and right about now they're seating the Gallegos party in my section. They're usually good for a two-hundred-dollar tab."

"You'll be fine. Don't worry. I mean, there're plenty of restaurants in this city."

"It's not that. It's looking for a job. It stinks, José. The applications, the interviews. I'm going to need references. What do you think Manny is going to say about me?"

"List me as a reference."

Nina sighed and took a sip of her drink. "Who knows? You'll probably be pounding the pavement right along with me."

"Hey." José grinned. "Today is my first time. It takes three times." He held up three fingers, mimicking Manny.

"Yeah, but you're the chef. And you walked out." She screwed the lid back on the bottle.

They continued down the street, José trying to figure out how to bring up the subject of Nina's pregnancy. He had come with her to talk about it and now they were doing anything but. His mother always knew what to do to draw him out when he had troubles. "You hungry?"

"I could eat," Nina said.

"I know a good place."

They stepped from the subway station back out onto the street. Nina hadn't traveled around the city this much in years. She'd become such a creature of habit. Home. Work. Home. Work. Nina picked at her uniform. "What am I going to do with this dress? Probably sell it on eBay."

José shrugged.

They continued down Houston Street and Nina longed to put her hand in his, not because she was feeling romantic, but because José knew her secret and that drew him to her somehow. But she held off. Everybody at the restaurant knew that José never went out with women. José was some kind of strange penitent, they said, but without the pilgrimages and glass in his shoes. Although, who knows, maybe he did have glass in his shoes. He'd been wearing the same pair ever since he started. Raggedy sneakers. One time she asked him why he never got new shoes, and he said shoes just weren't his thing anymore.

Weird.

No. No hand-holding. And maybe she was just feeling so unable to cope that she'd hold hands with Marilyn Manson if he were the day's companion.

She stole a glance at José.

Okay, no. Definitely not Marilyn Manson.

A man sat on the sidewalk, delicate origami pieces resting on boxes and crates: dragons and swans, hearts and butterflies and frogs. His blue eyes contrasted with his walnut skin, and a constellation of dark moles spotted his face. His gray T-shirt was darkened by dirt and grime and too much time on his back, but something about him told Nina he was a friend.

When he spoke, unable to meet her eyes, Nina realized he was blind.

"Can I interest you in one of my creations, young lady?" He held up an intricately folded creature. "How about this nice frog?"

How did he know she was a woman?

"I'm sorry. I don't have any cash on me."

And how much was something like that worth? To Nina, quite a bit. The man being blind surely added on twenty bucks or so, didn't it?

He rested his hands on his knees. "Okay." He nodded. "Today's a beautiful day, right?"

"I guess . . ."

"Describe it to me!" He smiled, nodding with an almost adolescent expectation.

"What?"

"Describe it to me and this piece of art is yours." He held out the frog again.

José nodded at her, his face open and almost as expectant as the blind man's.

"Okay. Uh . . ." She glanced over her shoulder at a

small park. "There are some yellow flowers blooming on a bu—"

"Forsythia!" He nodded.

In that instant, Nina knew this man wasn't born blind.

"Yeah. And some purple ones too—"

"Hyacinth!" He inhaled through his nose. "Mmm."

His face almost split in two at the joy of remembering those colors. Easter colors. She was feeding him, feeding his soul, like giving a man in the desert a drink of water.

"You really like flowers, huh?"

"Oh yeah."

She smiled at José.

"What's going on across the street?" the blind man asked.

She leaned forward, hands on her knees. "Well, it's just an ordinary day in New York City. People rushing back and forth. Everyone's got somewhere to go, somewhere to be. Nobody really cares about nothing. It's like a huge living clock. It never stops."

And why was she speaking so loudly? She caught herself and had to laugh inwardly. The man wasn't deaf!

His smile became wistful. "Boy, I wish I could see that."

Oh yes, you do, she thought. *I wish I could too.*

He handed her the frog. "Thank you."

She took it tenderly, wondering how she was going to keep something so fragile from being crushed. Well, she'd introduce him to Bubbles and maybe they'd have themselves a good old time there in her backpack.

"And you!" The blind man pointed to José. "You keep it real. I got my eye on you."

They laughed.

"Thank you," said Nina.

"Thank you," José said too.

As they walked on, Nina pointed to the sign resting beside the blind man, words scrawled in red magic marker, a little American flag sticker stuck to the cardboard:

GOD CLOSED MY EYES. NOW I CAN SEE.

"What do you think of that?" she asked José as they rounded the corner. "Did God do that to that man? Do you think he was being punished for something?"

José flinched. "I don't believe that of God." End of story, judging by the tone of his voice.

"I can't get mad at God for my being pregnant."

"No. Babies are like flowers."

Nina shut down that train of thought; she was actually thinking that she'd gotten herself into the mess. She wasn't talking about babies.

And all for Pieter. What was she thinking? He couldn't even stand up to Manny and tell him the truth when her job was on the line. It made her sick to think she'd slept with him.

She pointed to a street bazaar, tents set up, card tables all selling colorful items: purses, scarves, tablecloths, jewelry, batik and tie-dyed skirts and shirts, colorful sandals. And of course, watches. What street bazaar would be complete without fake Rolexes and, well, whatever other watch was popular these days? "Let's go over to the sidewalk vendors. I like that kind of hippie stuff."

"All right."

José followed her into a tent filled with skirts and blouses, dresses and scarves. Nina plucked a scarf from a rack, a soft square of white with sea-blue designs.

She walked up to the vendor. "Do you have a mirror?"

The Asian lady held one up while Nina tied the scarf around her head, her ponytail peeking out of the back. "Thank you."

She turned to José and tried her best Marlene Dietrich impersonation. "How do you do?"

She held out her hand to be kissed.

José just whistled.

Oh well.

"Looks pretty good, huh?" he said.

"Sure." She shrugged and took off the scarf.

"José?"

Nina turned and watched as a woman almost as tall as José, and as fair and beautiful as he was dark and handsome, wove through the crowd of shoppers. Her blonde hair moved about her head, cut perfectly. She looked like a model. She probably was one. Oh man. Didn't she know that it was Nina's day to have a crisis? That she didn't need to be standing next to Ms. Perfect and fall down flat in comparison?

A baby outfit, a cute little baseball-themed jumpsuit, hung on a hanger from her fingers. A size 0 *and* a mom? Life was completely unfair for a woman like that to show up on a day like today.

José whipped around at the sound of his name.

"Oh my gosh! José! It is you!"

"Helen." He'd thought about seeing her, but . . . not here. Not now.

She reached out, and he had no choice but to hug her in return. It felt so awkward. They'd broken up before the tragedy. She was wealthy, a soccer fan, and traveled all over the world to watch her favorite teams. They met one night after a match, at a bar near Wembly Stadium, and, well, he didn't want to think about it all right now. They'd had too much to drink.

"Look at you." She flipped a lock of hair just above his ear. "I barely recognized you under all this hair. How have you been? I haven't seen you in so long."

"Fine. I mean—"

How much did she know?

"Oh, I'm sorry. I heard about what happened to you, but the stories were so jumbled."

He couldn't talk about this now. He turned to Nina. "This is Nina. Nina, this is Helen."

Helen smiled. "Nice dress." She traced Nina's outfit with her light blue gaze. "You must really love Mexico, right?"

José winced. Helen could be such a snob. She didn't mean to be. She never meant anything badly, it just came out that way. Remarks like this had made José realize that, despite his status as a professional soccer player, he came from humble beginnings.

Nina smiled and José could see by the way her shoulder tried to meet her ear that she was uneasy. "It's my work uniform."

"Oh, where do you work?"

He was going to stop this, for Nina's sake. "We work for my brother."

Helen raised her brows. "Manny?"

"Mmm-hmm. I cook at his restaurant."

Helen crossed her arms. "What happened to your plans, weren't you signing with Club—"

"You know. Plans change."

Again. Clueless. Why would Helen begin to think he'd want to talk about that? And in front of Nina. She didn't know he and Nina weren't seeing each other.

Wait. Yes, she did.

Helen knew that José wouldn't have dated a humble waitress back in the old days. Trophy women, beautiful specimens of femininity were all he was interested in back then.

He wondered then what he might have been missing out on with such parameters.

"So you never played again?"

Take a hint, por favor.

"No. Something came up. We have to go. Good to see you."

He quickly paid for the scarf with the bills he had in his pocket. "Bye, Helen."

He grabbed Nina's hand and hurried her out of the tent. The quicker he left Helen behind the better, and unfortunately, she now knew where to find him.

José dropped her hand and gave her the scarf.

"Who was she?" Nina asked, lighting up a cigarette.

He didn't want to go through it with Nina. He pushed his hair out of his eyes. "Someone I used to see."

"Someone you used to see, hmm? Do you think I'm as pretty as she is?"

José looked at her. Why did women have to ask these kinds of questions? No, Nina wasn't nearly as pretty as Helen. But her face was kind and open, and her dark eyes flashed when she was angry. When she smiled she revealed straight teeth, and there was a vulnerability to Nina that sweetened her face like powdered sugar sweetens fresh strawberries. Helen was a crème brûlée. Fancy and highly prized but no good on a hot summer's day. He smiled at Nina.

She pulled the scarf off her head. "Of course not. She's prettier. So, someone you used to see. Boy, you are full of surprises."

Eleven

ina walked up to an ATM, slid in her card, and punched in her pin. She pulled out her cell phone and jiggled it from side to side at José. "I can't even keep a phone well fed. You know I had to get a cosigner for this thing?" She chose the Fast Cash twenty-dollar button. "That's how screwed up my credit is. And I could be picking up that big tip right now. Rent's due. I have to pay rent and bounce my last five hundred." *Not to mention my half of the clinic fee.*

The machine spat out the money; Nina grabbed it and stuffed it in her purse. "Hey, sorry I've been such a grump."

José looked at her quizzically. "What's a grump?"

Nina grabbed his arm. "It's when someone isn't being as nice as they should. Thanks for coming with me."

José just nodded and stood there, silent as usual.

She hiked her purse up on her shoulder. "So where we gonna eat?"

José said, "Let's get a taxi."

"Why don't we eat around here?"

"Patience, Nina. Let's get a cab."

A cab? José? "But I thought you don't ride in cabs."

More restaurant lore about José. They chalked it up to frugality, figuring he'd inherited some of that from Manny.

"That was yesterday."

"Okay. I'm tired anyway."

So they exchanged small talk while they waited for a vacant cab, Nina pulling information out of José who, she was sure, would have preferred to stand there in the continued silence. She tried to ask him questions with short answers.

José's favorite subject in school was math; Nina's was history. José's favorite color was blue; Nina's was orange. José's favorite ice cream was strawberry; Nina's was cookies and cream. José didn't watch television; Nina liked *Gilligan's Island*. José had wanted to be a doctor when he was really little; Nina wanted to be a dancer. She couldn't believe she blurted it out.

"A dancer? Really, Nina? What kind of dancer?"

He looked into her eyes, interested. Nina felt like somebody was really seeing her for the first time in years. "A Broadway dancer. Tap, jazz, modern. You know, shows."

"No ballet, huh?"

"I dunno. I guess for me, so much of dance is about the music. Classical is okay and I know there's modern ballet, but I like rhythm, José. I like it when the notes force themselves down into your heart and into your stomach and you can't help but respond with your body. I knew I wanted to dance as long as I could remember."

"So how do we get you dancing again?"

He looked so hopeful standing there, hands jammed deep in his pockets. Nina could see something different in José's eyes. "You're gonna help me decide about the pregnancy *and* get my career on track? Man, you've got your work cut out for you, don't you?"

A cab pulled up to the curb. José opened the door and helped her inside.

"So"—she slid over on the black vinyl seat—"we going to meet another mysterious person you used to *see*?"

He hesitated, then slid in next to her. "Frannie runs the Hacienda Sancho Panza." He gave the address to the driver, then white-knuckled the handle of the door. "You ever heard of it?"

Nina shook her head. "So. This Frannie . . ."

"Frannie was one of the first people I met when I came to this country."

"So she wouldn't go out with you?"

"No." He screwed up his face.

"Why not?"

"She said she liked me too much to ruin it."

Nina laughed. She was going to like Frannie.

"Think she'll ever settle down?"

José nodded. "Yes, but now she's married to her job."

"Maybe she'll meet someone in the restaurant. People who love the same things should end up together."

José just smiled. Apparently he had reached his maximum word count for the hour.

Well, I survived, he thought, climbing out of the cab. He'd tried to appear calm, but despite the fact the cabbie, African judging by his garb and accent, said he'd gone for fifteen years without an accident, José couldn't help grabbing the door handle and pushing an imaginary brake pedal on the floor. Thankfully Nina didn't notice.

It was surely an experience he hadn't missed. Truth was, it wasn't just cabs he avoided. He hadn't ridden in any car in over three years.

The Hacienda Sancho Panza spilled its aroma and some of its tables as well onto the sidewalk. Though cooking wasn't his first choice of vocation, it would have been had he no talent on the field. Truth was, he loved good food.

Since prison, he didn't allow himself all the luxuries he used to, but that was the beauty of food, particularly from his native Mexico. Even the simplest combinations formed the sublime. Chiles and onion and tomato. A man could create an empire with those three items.

Not that Manny wasn't trying.

He ushered Nina through the door and up to where the hostess stood behind her podium going over her tables. Their shadows fell across her seating chart and she glanced up, looked them up and down, taking in Nina's embroidered dress and José's chef's coat. He suddenly realized what this must look like and he wanted to laugh, but he stayed quiet, waiting to see how the situation developed. She was a beautiful woman, thin, like a willow tree. Just the sort he would have been interested in years ago.

"We only take applications on Tuesdays from three to five." She pursed her glossy lips and pushed a tassel of brown hair away from her forehead.

He leaned forward. "Um, can you please tell Frannie that José Suviran is here?"

She squinted, lowering her brows. "Regarding?"

"Just tell her I need to borrow a pound of saffron."

She was a class act, José thought, as she failed to lose her cool. "One moment please." She headed toward the kitchen, apparently oblivious to the fact that a pound of saffron was the equivalent of a football field of cultivation and would cost around five thousand dollars.

Nina burst into laughter.

José turned back toward the street where a little girl skipped, blonde pigtails bouncing as she kept up with her mother, holding her hand. A beautiful child, so much like—

"José," Nina called. "What are you looking at?"

And then Frannie burst from the kitchen doors dressed in a tailored yet feminine pantsuit, her dark hair streaked with blonde, corkscrewing around her head. "I can't believe it!"

She was a beautiful woman too. How could he have been around so many beautiful women and ended up so lonely? Even now, sweet Nina beside him, he had no desire to ask for her company in any way other than friendship.

"José! What a surprise!" Perfect teeth, expressive eyes. José wondered . . . no. Too much water under the bridge now.

"How are you doing, Frannie?"

"Better than you, José." She ran a finger along his bandaged hand. "You had one of these on last time I saw you. Don't tell me it's the same injury."

"No, no."

"Kitchen's a dangerous place. You boys burning each other again?" She laughed. José thought about the burn marks on his arm. Ones he didn't give himself. If customers knew what went on in the kitchens of the restaurants they ate at, they'd be shocked. Touch a man's broiler pans and you could end up scarred for life. Don't get near a grumpy man's grill, he'd warn them.

"No, Frannie."

"Well, it's always good to see the man with the mysterious beard. Don't tell me you really came thirty blocks for saffron?"

"No, we came here to eat. This is my friend Nina."

Frannie smiled, took the pencil from the hostess, and began making adjustment to the seating chart for José and Nina. "So, just taking the day off then?" She looked Nina up and down just like Helen had. "Nice dress. Let me guess. It was Manny's idea. It must have cost him a fortune."

Nina shook her head. "He made us pay for them."

Frannie stretched her mouth in a stiff smile. "Well, I would too."

Oh, the fraternity of it all. Frannie knew word would get back to Manny. Somehow. The woman knew how to cover her backside. José couldn't help but appreciate that quality in a person.

Frannie turned to the hostess and tapped a table in the diagram with her pen. "Give them table six, Margaret. When these people get here, give them table three and comp them a bottle of Penascal. The Landrys aren't due for another half hour. Plenty of time."

Margaret couldn't get over her shock. "But—"

"Oh, and these two—they can have anything under a buck fifty."

José bowed. Frannie could afford a lot more, but okay.

"Okay, make it two-fifty if you give me your mole recipe."

"Frannie, you know they'd kill me."

"Manny would, you mean." She tapped the podium. "Margaret, just tell Johannes to bring me the check."

Margaret led them to a table outside.

Nina settled herself and picked up a menu. Opposite her, José pulled his chair closer to the table as he sat down. "You like paella?"

"Oh yeah."

He took the menu from her and laid it on top of his.

The waiter stepped up to their table. "Good afternoon. My name is Johannes. Can I start you off with something other than water?"

"We're ready to order. We'll have your mejillones and paella for two."

"Very good," the waiter said. "Anything to drink?"

José thought about it. Why not? It was turning into a day of surprises. "Half soda, half lemonade, and add some fresh mint, please."

"Sounds fancy," said Nina.

After he left, José leaned forward. "Paella is full of the things you need for a child."

Whoa. Nina bristled. "Who said I was having a child?"

"You did."

"No. I said I was pregnant."

The waiter returned, setting down their drinks.

"I'm not ready to have a kid. If you have a kid, your freedom's gone."

Not to mention your sanity, your privacy.

"Things change," José said.

Oh, lovely. Thanks for that. "Having a kid isn't just a *change*. I don't think I even like children. I've hardly been around any, José."

He just nodded.

So she kept babbling. "I just can't do it. I'm broke and alone."

"Alone?"

There. She'd said it. Alone. Pregnant and alone, and that equaled only one thing. Pathetic loser. His eyes searched hers and in them was mirrored the sadness she felt so deeply at that moment. How had she landed here? In this place? Pregnant, jobless, boyfriendless, sitting in a strange restaurant with a man whose beard was the size of Staten Island, and to top it off, wearing a dress no other woman in New York would dare wear in public.

Down in her backpack, the paper frog and Bubbles rode on a pair of Converse tennis shoes. She wondered if there was a special kind of shoe that you could just put on and run, run fast and hard, run away from your life. And if she thought life was hard now, what about with some baby along for the ride?

No thanks.

And there it sat.

"I made my decision. Okay?"

"So what does the father think?"

"He's not a father, and he's not going to be a father. Just like I'm not going to be a mother. Not now." Now was not the time to talk about Pieter. Who—she looked down at her phone—had not called one time to see how she was doing since he handed over her belongings. Figured. "He is all for 'getting it taken care of.' Those are the words he used. As if it was a wisdom tooth to be pulled out." She leaned toward José, wanting him to get the message. "You know, I wonder why kids are always the problem of the mother? Guys aren't inconvenienced by them. They don't ruin their freedom. And yet they have all this advice about what's best for me."

"What guys, Nina?"

But she was on a roll. "Well, taking care of it is what's best for me." How could he possibly understand? "Put yourself in my shoes."

"Do you love him?"

What happened to the quiet José who minded his own business?

"I don't." She couldn't help herself. It had been so long

since somebody actually sat and listened to her. "It's Pieter's baby," she whispered.

José's eyes grew, their whites showing beneath his dark lashes. "I didn't know."

"Nobody did. It was all a big mistake, and Manny . . ."

"Yes. He would have fired you both if he knew."

"And what happens when I find someone I do love? With a kid?" Oh, she could picture it. "Forget it. I invite someone up for a nightcap . . . and pay off the babysitter?" She tapped her fingers on the tabletop. "Mr. Right is gonna say, 'Oh yeah, I love taking care of other people's children.' It's hard enough"—she gulped back the lump in her throat—"to get people's sincerity without throwing kids into the mix."

She shook her head. No, no, no. She just couldn't picture all the bottles, the diapers, the 3:00 a.m. feedings, and dropping the kid off at day care. Little jammies and socks. "I can't even take care of myself, José. How am I going to take care of a kid?"

José reached out and settled his bandaged hand on Nina's forearm. The sight of it, for the staff knew what he'd been doing to himself for so long, undid her. This wounded soul reaching out, his own pain somehow a comfort to her . . . and she cried. For the first time since those blue lines marred the snowy surface of the test stick, the fear of life, the giving of it, the taking of it, the living of it, overwhelmed her completely.

Twelve

Manny looked at the clock on the wall. Only forty-five minutes until the rush would be over. They hadn't had a lunch rush like this in a month, and today just had to be the day.

Not good.

The waitstaff milled about the window as the kitchen staff tried to plate food and get it ready to be served.

Manny handed Nina's replacement a plate. "Here, you're done, you're done." He set another one on the window. "Here, that's yours."

Pieter returned a plate to the window.

"What's this?" Manny asked. "What's wrong with that plate?"

"They sent it back."

"What do you mean, 'They sent it back'?"

"They said it was cold."

Manny could almost feel the top of his head unhinging so the steam could fly out of his skull. "It's cold?"

The phone rang.

Perfect.

"Somebody better go get the phone. I better not hear more than two rings, people. Somebody better go get the phone!"

More servers milled around him, more cooks, more, more, more. He handed a plate to a waiter whose name he couldn't remember. "Here. It's on the house, okay. Table two."

"What about my order?" a young woman asked. Who was she? Manny didn't recognize her. Pieter usually okayed every hire with him. Maybe he was getting a little too cocky.

"I'm waiting for the special."

He turned to Pepito. "Where's the snapper? Give me that snapper."

Pepito shook his head. "This isn't for her!"

"It's for Mr. Winters," said the waitress.

"Make a new one!" Manny shouted, grabbing the snapper from Pepito and handing the plate to her.

"Here. Take this out. Table ten. And tell Mr. Winters I love his shoes, okay?"

Pepito snorted.

Manny turned to him. "Don't give me that look. I do not need that look today."

Frannie approached them as they finished up their mussels. She turned around a chair from the vacant table behind them, straddled the seat, and sat down with her arms draped across the backrest. "You two doing all right? How were the mussels?"

José airplaned his hand back and forth. "Good."

"But?"

"Try to use Pinot Grigio in the broth instead."

Frannie smiled at Nina and shrugged. "Is he like this back at Manny's?"

"He's the *chef* at Manny's. We had a sub today," she said.

José set down his fork. "I really like the direction you've taken the place."

"You like it? Then the kitchen's yours. When do you start?"

"How about a package deal?" He pointed to Nina. And why not? Frannie and he had been doing favors for one another for a long time.

She turned to Nina. "You looking? I know this guy won't ever come down. But if you're looking, we could use someone. And if he recommends you . . ."

"I recommend her."

Nina's eyes widened; half her mouth rose in a smile.

"Ring me on Monday."

A food runner sidled up to the table with a tray.

Frannie tapped the back of the chair, then stood. "Okay, I'm going to let you guys eat."

"Thank you," Nina said. "I'll call you. It was nice to meet you."

"Nice to meet you too."

"Frannie, gracias." José knew she'd come through. And she'd do right by Nina. Frannie was a woman of integrity, even if she did work too hard.

Frannie grinned and José knew that grin. "De nada." She'd expect something in return, and he knew just what he was going to give her.

José turned to Nina after Frannie left. "See? That was easy."

Nina teared up again.

Must be the pregnancy, José thought.

"What are you doing the rest of the day, Nina?"

"Dealing with this."

"Do you want to go to the beach with me? I want to show you something."

He had to get her there. Something in him that loved the sand, the crash of the waves, and the scream of the gulls reached out to Nina and told him she'd understand him there and he'd understand her and maybe she could find another way. Maybe they both could. Plus, his family would be there.

She hesitated. "Okay. But I want to get out of these crazy clothes."

"We can go like this." Of course, he wasn't the one in that loud skirt.

Nina sighed. "Why not?"

"But first, I have to go back to the restaurant to get my wallet."

"You mean you came here without your wallet?"

"I know Frannie. She'd never let me pay." José downed his water, then spread out his napkin. "You got a pen, Nina?"

She nodded and dug one out of her backpack. "What are you doing?"

"Watch."

He scribbled down the words *Mole Verde de Oaxaca* followed by the ingredients to his mole sauce, and Nina's eyes widened. "Manny's gonna kill you!"

"Manny will never find out because Frannie would not tell him. Will you?"

"Of course not."

Ten minutes later Johannes approached the table. "Is that everything?"

"Almost." José handed him the napkin. "Frannie's been bugging me for this for years. See what you can get for it."

Johannes bowed his head and smiled. "I will, sir. Thank you. You both have a great day."

Nina pulled a twenty out of her purse and set it on the table. Waitstaff respect. José admired it. She didn't have much money, he knew.

"And tell Frannie it's not all about the ingredients."

José watched the scene in the kitchen before making his presence known. There was Kevin, Manny's favorite waiter, holding one dirty plate, while Margarita, whose name Manny could never remember, lugged a large tray of dirty dishes.

Carlos snorted. "Pacing yourself there, Kevin?"

"These were the only dishes in my section, okay?"

Carlos glared at him, and José figured now was as good a time as any to make his presence known. He walked forward, patting Carlos, then Pepito, on the back. They returned the gesture in kind, welcoming him back.

Pieter entered, placed his hands on his hips. "Did you have a good day off, José?"

José wanted more than anything to grab him by the lapels and give him a shaking like he'd never experienced. He'd never had much respect for Pieter, who was always trying to antagonize him, but knowing what he did magnified everything negative about the man. Still, he wanted to keep Nina's confidence. "I've had a great day, Pieter. Nina is a wonderful person." He glared at him.

Pieter called toward the line, "Hey, Manny! Your brother's back," then sidled behind Carlos.

José figured he better just make for the lockers.

"Hey, El Callao! Where you been, man?" Carlos asked.

"Was it busy?" He slid his phone off the counter.

"Oh man." Carlos wiped his sweating brow with a red bandana. "Oh man, it's been crazy. We did the best we could."

"Two tables walked out on us," Pieter said, almost looking happy about it if it meant José was in trouble.

What was this? Second grade?

Manny stormed into the kitchen. "You just sneaking in and out? You weren't going to say hello?"

"I just came to pick up my phone and wallet, Manny."

Manny breathed through his nose, and his words issued through his teeth. "Yes . . . you forgot your phone. I called you. Mama called you too. I found time to call you." And it was suddenly too much for him. José watched with awe as the dam of self-control gave way and his brother unloaded. "Even though we were short one chef during our lunch rush hours! Where were you, José, huh?"

"I just went outside, Manny. That's all I was planning to do."

There was no way Nina was going to go back into the restaurant, so she waited outside instead.

She lit up a cigarette. She wasn't a big-time smoker, only when life became a little stressful. *Why am I doing this? I don't even look like a real smoker.*

Nina hated things like this about herself. Relying on silly stuff like cigarettes and stupid guys like Pieter.

And there was José inside, trying to be a good friend and a nice guy. She knew he wanted to tell her a thousand different reasons to keep her baby, but for some reason he couldn't, as if he didn't have the right. But he listened to her, and she couldn't remember the last time somebody really did that for her.

Sometimes Manny didn't understand his brother. "You went outside? Marcos took some trash out. He didn't see you outside. How far outside did you go, hermano, huh? Acapulco? Where were you? We were worried. We were busy and you bailed on us." He jabbed a finger in José's chest. "You abandoned your own flesh and blood!"

José just needed to see sense. There, the mop. Manny grabbed it and shoved it toward his brother. "Here. You can make this up to me by cleaning up this mess! You're lucky I don't cut the whole staff and let you do it by yourself!"

He walked away. Let José stew for a while.

"Manny! Manny!" José called.

He turned, feeling the lion of anger return. He knew what José was going to say because José was his brother and they knew these things.

"I just came for my stuff. I have to do this now, Manny." He handed Manny the mop.

Manny threw the mop in the corner, knocking over a stack of cans. "What? What do you have to do?"

"I have to go."

"What?!" Manny wanted to strangle him.

The kitchen fell silent. The water stopped running. Knives stilled. People leaned in their direction. Manny looked around. "What's everyone staring at? We have work to do." He pointed at José. "*You!* In my office. Right now!"

He would settle this immediately. As mad as he was, he couldn't let his brother leave without him seeing things correctly.

Besides, dinner prep needed to begin pronto.

José followed Manny down the steps to the office. Manny could think what he wanted about José's Spartan lifestyle, his cloistered ways, but Manny's life revolved around the restaurant. It was a different kind of cloister. And even now, one of his former employees was in trouble, but as he saw it, she was out there and they were in here.

José knew it was time to take a stand.

Manny's eyes blazed. "I called everyone. I called Mama and Papa. You left all of us when you walked out that door with your new friend."

Mama and Papa. Manny . . .

"Two tables walked out on us today, José! *Two!* That's never happened. Never. This is bad business, José, bad business."

That's right, José realized. This wasn't about family at all. "Everything to you is business. I'm sure everyone picked up the slack and got you and your restaurant through the day. But what are you doing for them?"

Manny clenched his jaw. "Wait, wait, wait. Am I hearing this correctly?" He pointed toward the door. "Ask Amelia. She's been here the whole time. She has four kids and commutes from the Bronx every day."

"She has three kids, Manny."

"She has kids!"

"See? You don't even know her and you're giving the Amelia speech to me? How long have you been running this place? And how many times have you given Amelia a raise?" He made an O with his fingers. "*Zero*, Manny. Zero."

José watched his brother's nostrils flare. Better just to get out of there. He turned.

"Listen to me, niñito. Don't tell me how to run my business. You work for me, and walk out on me? Your brother? The one who bailed you out and employed you?"

José felt his heart speed up, anger running up from the base of his spine to flare over his head. "Manny . . . ," he warned.

"You just leave me for some late, drunk waitress? When did this happen?"

José was finished. He loved his brother, but Manny could jump to conclusions so quickly. And dragging up the past like he'd done? He'd had enough.

"You fired a pregnant woman, Manny."

He stormed back to the kitchen.

Manny punched the wall in his office. José had heard that sound before.

And then the subsequent pounding of his feet as he rushed up the steps. José sighed. So this wasn't over yet. And poor Nina, waiting outside through all of this. He hoped she'd still be there.

Manny grabbed José's arm. "I didn't know why she was late! All I knew was that she was late all the time!"

"And you know she wasn't always like that." He pushed his hair back with a sigh. "Manny, she's one of your best employees. Been here for four years. You ever stop to ask her what was going on?" José pointed to everyone around them. "You know anything about any of these people besides Amelia?"

He might as well go all the way. He breathed in deeply. "You know anything more than the fact that Henry the bartender is making twice as much as Pepito, my *cook*? Why does Pieter always give better sections to Kevin than Margarita?"

"Enough!" Manny straightened his tie and looked around him, a flush seeping from his collar up to his hairline. He pushed José toward the walk-in freezer and shut the door behind them.

Manny pushed José's shoulder. *"What's wrong with you? How do you get away with talking like that in front of my employees?"*

It always came down to pride with Manny. *"What's wrong with me? What's wrong with you, man? What is it with you? What is it?"* José pushed Manny back. *"Carlos, Carlos, one of your people, he's below minimum wage, man. Why is that, huh? Oh, he doesn't have papers? And you can get away with it?"* He pushed open the door. *"We all slave in the kitchen for you. It's* all about you, man!"

José stormed out of the walk-in. Time to get out of here. *"Enough of this talk about family,"* he mumbled.

Manny followed. "José!"

José picked up a pot on the counter and turned on Manny. "This pot is the same one you bought eight years ago when you opened. It scorches because it's old." He pushed the pot into Manny's chest. "Buy another one."

José cruised by Kevin, then by Pieter, staring a hole into him. "You got something to say?" he asked Pieter.

Pieter's face paled.

If he could say one more thing . . . no. He'd already become angry enough. There was no telling what he'd do to Pieter once he got started.

"You clean out your locker too! I'm done!" Manny hollered.

José stopped, looked at his brother, and waved him off with a weary hand. He was done too. He couldn't get out of there fast enough.

"And call Mama. She's worried."

I'll bet she is, José thought.

Thirteen

Nina ground out the half-smoked cigarette beneath her heel. She wasn't planning to keep this baby, but just in case . . . pregnancy or not, it wasn't good to smoke, right? She had to rely on something other than cigarettes to get through the rest of this day. She stepped into a nearby convenience store to buy some snacks for the trip to the beach.

Several minutes later, apples and water in her bag, she waited back at her post, only imagining how Manny must have been reaming out his brother.

José, hands balled up into clenched fists, pale with anger, stormed out of the restaurant, and right into traffic. Nina watched in horror as the driver of a maroon sedan jammed on his breaks and yelled out the window, "Hey, man! What are you tryin' to do?"

José stared at him, blinking, suddenly far away from the scene.

Where did you go? Where do you go when that happens? she wondered.

José shook his head and came to life again.

She met him as he stepped up onto the curb. "Are you all right? What happened?"

José shook his head, eyes moist. "Let's go."

"Don't tell me he fired you!"

He just stared at her. Oh no.

"I can't believe him! He is such a piece of—"

"He's been good to me."

Okay, fine. Family loyalty and all that. She got it. She adjusted her purse. "I guess we did ruin his day." She held up a shopping bag, made it a peace offering of sorts. "Got some things for the trip."

"Let's go."

"Did Pieter say anything?"

"No."

"Did you say anything to him about me?"

"No. But I'm sure he guessed I knew."

That was okay with Nina. Let Pieter squirm a little bit. He deserved to.

"Let's get a train. I'm ready for the beach after all of that."

"Okay," Nina said.

They made their way to Penn Station. Nina thought about her decision. She could hardly blame this baby for canceling out her dreams. And she could hardly say it would keep her from reaching her goals. She'd done that on her own. It wasn't going to be easy. Today would end and there'd be another day to make the *real* decision.

They waited at a crosswalk near the station.

"When did you know you wanted to be a dancer?" José asked.

That was easy. "It was my father. He could cut quite the rug."

"Excuse me?"

"American expression. He could really dance himself."

"Your father, eh? Not your mother?"

"No. She's the more quiet type. Sometimes I wondered how they ended up together. My father was from the South and he loved dancing and parties. My mom just wanted to be home with her 'little family,' as she always called us." The light changed, and they crossed the street. "I knew I wanted to dance when my father told me one day that I had the prettiest arms he'd ever seen—"

"You have nice arms."

"Thanks. And he told me I moved them gracefully." She kicked up a foot. "My feet too."

José took her elbow as they stepped off the curb.

"So, he asked if I wanted lessons, and after that first one, I just knew. Sometimes you feel like you were made to do something, be somebody."

"Yes, I know."

They stepped up onto the opposite curb, skirting around a group of people waiting for cabs.

They entered the station.

"Maybe, you go back and start dancing again."

"Not pregnant, I can't." There, let him chew on that.

"Afterward."

"After what?"

"After you have the baby."

They stopped by the ticket booth.

"I told you—"

"Yes, I know." He put a couple of twenties on the counter. "Two tickets for Long Island."

Now this was a better train ride. José looked past Nina and out the window. He didn't like subways much, but trains were another story altogether. The rhythm of the wheels on the tracks, the way the car swayed slightly, the soothing quality of scenery going by for you to see without the distraction of driving.

Not that he'd driven for a long time. Not since that day.

He closed his eyes.

"I could really use a bath and some Marvin Gaye." Nina's voice brought him around.

"You can take a bath at my parents'. They have Tito Puente. I don't know about Marvin Gaye."

"I thought we were going to the beach."

"They live at the beach."

"And they probably know what happened at Manny's today."

"Don't worry."

Nina settled herself more comfortably in her seat. "Oh, I don't worry. I used to worry, then I did a little research and I found out that ten out of ten people die." She laid her hands on the armrest. "Do you think that is all there is? That we only live once?"

"Well, so far I haven't met anyone who's lived twice."

There, that made her smile. Good. The beach was a good idea.

"Nina, can I ask you a question?"

"No."

He looked down at his hands. Well, okay.

"I'm kidding!" She laughed. "What?"

"Nothing."

"Just ask!"

Might as well just say it. This was what the day was supposed to be about. "Have you thought about adoption?"

"Do we have to talk about this right now?"

"No."

She looked out the window, then back at José. "I can't carry around a living thing inside of my body for nine months and then—what? Leave it on a doorstep in a basket for some stranger? To me, that's worse than anything."

"It doesn't have to be a stranger."

Nina grated out a laugh. "So I just start calling up my relatives? My *relative*? 'Hey, Mom, I haven't talked to you in five years, but I got something for you!' Or how about this? *You* can have it. I bet Manny could teach it a thing or two. The Suviran boys can raise little Nina because right now you're probably the only one in the world I trust."

There. That should quiet him down. Put a little of the responsibility on him and see how far it goes from there on out. Maybe he'd head to the clinic with her next Wednesday. She didn't know if she even wanted that, but going alone would be horrible. Somebody had to know in case she started bleeding afterward or something.

She reached into the bag and pulled out a tart, green apple. Granny Smith. She handed it to José.

"Thank you," he said.

"You're welcome." Might as well have one too. Amazing how people continued to breathe, walk, ride trains, eat apples, when their lives were falling apart.

The landscape sped by. Industrial buildings choked with smoke, and she hated cities so much. Why come to dance and then stay when the dream faded? That was silly. She bit into the apple. He bit into his again. Back and forth the sounds of their chomping cut the silence between them.

It was nice.

"Do you want to dance again?" José asked.

"It's been a long time. I'm not conditioned."

"I think you could do it."

Nina shook her head. "I believe you do."

She needed someone to believe in her. It had been so long.

An hour later, they exited the train at the Hampton station. Nina wished she could have grown up at the beach. Memories of her father filled her.

"Nina! Nina!"

Oh. She'd turned the wrong way.

José put an arm around her waist and directed her toward the stairs. They climbed up toward the sunlight and the smell of salty air.

Fourteen

The rusty gate to the front yard creaked in the wind, open to the street. "Loochi!"

Celia ran, her shoes pounding the heated cement, sending the jarring contact up her spine to the base of her skull.

And brakes squealed, and her child screamed, and a dull thump echoed across the face of the buildings.

Oh, God. A silence settled the air in an instant.

And Celia knew. She ran through the open gate. And Lucinda lay on the black road, limp. She threw aside the camera as the heat of fear slammed down onto her. "Loochi! No! No!"

She ran to her child, barely noticing the shiny black car. "No! Oh no!" she screamed, kneeling down next to

Lucinda, the blood fanning from the little body out into the street, a river, a crimson river eating Celia alive, consuming her life, everything.

She could barely breathe.

"Somebody call an ambulance! Somebody help me!" She pressed her ear to the tiny chest. Nothing, not a sound.

Oh no. Oh, God! Please!

The face, so pale. The ponytails askew. No.

Loochi. Oh my baby.

The driver appeared, his face pale, his eyes drowned in shock. Celia turned on him. "No! You!" she screamed, raising her fists and beating him as he took her into his arms. "No," she moaned. "No."

He whispered into her hair, trying to calm her.

"No! Oh no!" She pushed away from him and took Lucinda into her arms. Feeling the tiny bones of her daughter's legs and arms fall against her own.

But something overtook her at the sight of Lucinda's face. Dead and dead and dead. And a great groaning released from her core, accompanied by the oceans and oceans of love once destined to be released in gentle lappings, now spilled all at once onto her daughter, the street, the car, and the people now gathered on the sidewalk as she melted quickly into what all parents pray they'll never become.

Fifteen

They walked from the train station to José's house. Nina tasted the salty air as she inhaled through her nose, feeling that jangling roominess one experiences upon leaving the city for the first time in months. No tall buildings loomed overhead blocking air and sunshine, and vistas that reached farther than the next block.

See, she thought, *dancing is a little like this, a bit of spaciousness and freedom in a world where only those who can are allowed it.* And she could. She could move her feet and sway her arms gracefully, that taut yet somehow fluid arc of movement. It wasn't with pride she thought about it, but with a sense of accomplishment.

Well, she used to feel that way anyway. She hadn't danced a step in a year. Every once in a while she stretched in front of the TV, but that was the extent of it there in her cramped apartment.

She breathed in again, louder this time.

"This is good?" José asked.

"Yes. I don't know why I don't get out of the city more."

"I think we all say that."

"The city is no place to raise a child." Nina thought about the test strip and suddenly her life had become so important once again, as if all the things she'd stripped away of her own volition were back in play and in danger of being stripped away again by unwelcome circumstances.

"The fact is, I'm not a dancer, and I wasn't in danger of becoming one with the way my life worked out." *Okay, that was a little random*, she thought, but José didn't seem to notice. He just kept walking along, hands in his pockets, breathing in the sea air just like she did.

She continued forward past well-kept houses and thick lawns bearing springtime flowers, some obviously in some sort of yard war. Nina never saw such perfection.

They rounded a corner and came upon a yard with more lawn ornaments than she'd ever seen. "I like those kinds of people. They don't realize that lawn ornaments aren't classy. They just like them. Nobody ever told them 'less is more' so they think more is more, and the more lawn ornaments the better. I'd like to be that person, José. I'd like to not care what other people think."

"You don't seem like that."

"Maybe not to you."

They came to an intersection, and José pointed across the street to a white Dutch colonial with a perfect yard. "There it is. That is my parents' house."

"Okay . . ."

"Don't worry." He took her arm as they crossed the street. "You will love it here."

A man came barreling down the drive with an empty handcart. He stopped at the back of a red pickup filled with shrubbery.

"Qué paso, Papá?"

The man turned. His black eyes widened, then filled with concern. A flood of Spanish came out of his mouth as they approached. Nina felt a sick wave of uncertainty mix with the sea air.

Of course his father was surprised. José hadn't been home since he moved into the city to work at Manny's restaurant. It seemed he could only be one place at a time, live one life, and traveling out to Long Island regularly was not part of that life. His life was sleeping, praying, going to church, cooking, and coming home to read and sleep. That was enough. In fact, sometimes if the resolve it took to accomplish all that gave any indication, he was downright heroic.

Manuel Suviran Sr., olive skin weathered from days outside on his ranch in Mexico, spat out his worry. José felt badly that Nina wouldn't understand, but his father refused to speak English. *"José, where have you been? Your brother's been calling all day. He said you walked out."* He looked at Nina and then back at his son. *"What's happening, Son?"*

José replied in kind. They all suspected Manuel understood more than he let on, but they respected him too much to push the language issue. *"I'll tell you later."*

"Is everything all right?"

"Don't worry, old man."

His father embraced him. When most of his friends decided they were too old for hugs, their fathers acquiesced, but not Manuel. He saw it through.

"Remember Nina?" José asked. *"From the restaurant?"*

"Well, of course!" He turned to Nina with a little bow. *"This is your home."*

Nina looked back up at the tidy home, so neat and well cared for, and José was proud. "It's beautiful," she said.

"At your service."

Nina tried replying in Spanish. "Gracias."

He laughed. *"Listen to her. With that dress she looks like a real Mexican lady!"*

Nina drew her brows together. "What did he say?"

"He said you look like a Mexican."

She smiled. "Oh, thank you!"

José reached for a bush. Looked like an azalea. *"Is Mom inside?"*

"No. She went shopping. I'm going to cook an oyster plate. You're staying for dinner, right?"

"He's inviting us to dinner," José said to Nina. "Should we stay? He's making oysters."

"Sí. Gracias," Nina said.

José nodded. *"Sí. If you insist."*

Manuel spread his hands. *"Of course I insist."*

"What are the trees for, Papa?"

"To plant them, beard man. Don't just stand there like a lump! Yes. Three male sons and none of them can help me plant a tree."

"Where's Eduardo?" José asked.

Manual laid his hands on the root-ball of a small tree. *"Eduardo? You're joking. He's too busy buying clothes and wooing his new girlfriend."*

"He has a new girlfriend? When did that happen?"

"You know your brother. I haven't met her either. He's bringing her for dinner tonight."

José leaned against the side of the truck. It had been several months since he'd seen Eduardo. *"Good, I'll get to meet her. Is he here?"*

"No. Just me."

José pushed off the truck. *"Let's get these trees in the ground then. Nina's as strong as Eduardo."* He turned to Nina. "Aren't you, Nina?"

She scrunched up her nose. "What?"

Manuel hefted the root-ball, and José rushed to help him put the tree on the cart. *"The holes are done, we only need to plant them,"* he said.

"What are we doing?" Nina asked.

"He said he wants you off his property."

She looked at him through her lashes. "Cut it out." Then smiled. Then sobered. "Did he really say that?"

José couldn't help it. That smile was infectious. He returned the grin to reassure her. "Seriously, we're just going to help plant these trees." Wow, did José actually crack a joke?

José helped his father unload the rest of the plants while Nina set her backpack on the back porch.

"The Prodigal Son returns. Your mom will be so happy to see you."

José gripped the handle of the cart with Nina and pointed to his father. "He's gonna help us plant these trees, all right?"

Manuel laughed, joined in on the lighthearted banter. *"You're slower than a one-legged man."*

They stopped by the back fence.

Manuel spread his arms to indicate his living canvas. *"There're going to be azaleas, a lemon tree, tuberoses, irises, margaritas . . . it will be paradise!"*

Nina nodded.

"Did you understand that?" José asked.

She shook her head.

"You know," Manuel continued, "I wooed my wife with flowers. You like flowers?"

"What did he say?" she asked José.

"He asked if you like flowers."

She nodded, this smile wider than the one before it. *This must be doing her good*, he thought. "Yes. I do. I love flowers."

José was reasonably sure Pieter rarely brought her flowers. He thought Nina was smarter than to go for a guy like Pieter.

"See?" Manuel said. "All women like flowers!"

They dug into the black earth, turning over the moist soil with their shovels. And they planted the lemon trees, José and his father hefting the heavy plants and settling them in the holes while Nina packed the soil around them. Next they planted three azalea bushes and the rest of the perennials Manuel had brought home with him.

"You see, Nina"—Manuel patted the earth back into place around an iris—"right now these plants are small and just a shadow of what they will be."

José translated.

"This garden will be amazing in a few years," she said.

"Gardening! Food for the soul," Manuel said. "Let's take a break."

He came back with some cold drinks and sat on the cool grass. José and his dad talked about nothing really, but Nina seemed to drink it in. Finally they drained their glasses.

José said, *"Dad, do you have the keys to my car?"*

Manuel hesitated, closing his eyes.

Nina noticed, giving José a look of curiosity.

"The keys? What for, son?"

"I want to show it to Nina."

Manuel looked at Nina, then back at José. In his gaze José read a three-hour conversation. Why her? Is there something you're not telling us? Are you in trouble? Are you healing? Are you ready to get on with your life? And if so . . . why her? *"They are in the bottom drawer of my desk."* He stood up. *"I'm going to shower and change."*

José sipped his drink.

"What just happened?" Nina asked.

José shook his head. "Nothing."

He thought about the women he used to bring home and wondered if they would think Nina was a step down. He hoped not. Truthfully, the more time he spent with her, the more he liked her, the more he hoped she'd find somebody who appreciated her more than Pieter had. Of course, knowing who Pieter was, that wouldn't be too hard to do.

Nina entered the carport. Something hung in the air, and she wasn't sure what it was. But it seemed important, weighty, and full of consequence. She wasn't very religious, but it felt almost like a shrine of sorts.

A car ran down the middle of the room filling up almost the entire space, a dustcloth draped over most all of it. José began to remove it. Nina ran her forefinger down the front fender, the only part exposed. Her finger cut through the dust of many years.

She loved old cars, and this Bel Air was a beauty. Sleek and old but in perfect condition. "Wow! Does it run?"

José stood on the other side of the car, by the driver's door. He removed the last bit of tarp with a flick of his wrists. "Let's see."

Nina hopped in, jumping onto the passenger's seat. Cars were so big and roomy back in the day; it was almost like entering a theater box. Could she imagine Pieter in something like this? Something unusual, something fun? No way. "My dad used to have an old Ford."

Oh no, he's gone again, she thought, looking over at José, who gripped the steering wheel as if searching for a port in a storm. After just half a day with him, she wished she could share some of that heavy load. Even just a pound or two if he'd let her.

"Is it yours?"

José looked up. "Yeah."

"Wow."

He slid the key into the ignition.

Nina decided to make this fun. She had no idea why this car was important, why it had the power to steal José away, but maybe she had the power to bring him back. She pulled the scarf out of her pocket. "I've got the scarf." Placing it around her head, she thought about all those old movies she used to watch with her mom, movies where Grace Kelly, the most beautiful woman in the world as far as she was concerned, tied on a headscarf, set a pair of sunglasses on her nose, and headed off down a windy, coastal road. "We should take a road trip across the country."

He turned the key, the result a series of rapid clicks.

"Doesn't look like you drive this much."

"I used to."

"When was the last time you drove this thing?"

"Last time I drove it, I went to jail."

Oh boy, she thought. *Here it is.*

She didn't know if she was ready.

Sixteen

José figured Nina was in his life for a purpose. Yes, he cared about her and what happened to her baby, but he also knew that he needed help every bit as much as she did. Maybe more. Because at the end of the day, Nina was strong. Whereas he, well, he wanted to be. He used to be.

"You went to jail?" She took off the scarf. "For what?"

He remembered the day, driving down the street with Francisco, having just given the practice ball to the boys in the street, promising to bring back their raggedy ball with a newfound wealth of signatures along its seams.

"About six years ago, I was on my way to a press conference. I had just signed a contract with a new soccer team."

"You played soccer?"

José nodded.

From professional soccer player to hermit chef?

"What happened?"

"Everything happened so fast. We were driving down the street, and I had just bought new shoes so I lifted up my foot to show Francisco, my manager."

They had joked about a foot massage, and José looked down at the shoes, remembering how he'd promised himself years before that the first thing he'd buy when he had the money was a pair of Ferragamos. And he had them. All that money he had plunked down on the counter.

And now they were riding down the street, laughing about the shoes, cigar smoke flying in the breeze from the convertible.

"We're moving up," Francisco had said.

"I think I'm lost," José said, looking around.

"It's the next right."

Why did it have to be that street? Any other that day and it would have been fine.

"Those shoes come with the car?" Francisco asked.

José lifted his foot, patting the sole of the shoe. They stood for everything he had worked so hard for. Every practice after school when his friends were hanging out together, every break spent kicking balls in the rain, every holiday interrupted by more practice. And all the running, miles and miles each day.

Yes. He looked at his shoes and satisfaction ran through him like an electrical current.

He heard a cry. And then a thump.

José jammed on the breaks.

There was nothing in front of the car. That they could see.

"Was that a dog?" Franciso asked.

They looked at each other, terrified. José knew. His heart told him it was more than an alley cat or a roaming, stray dog. *"What do we do?"* he asked his manager.

"Let's get out of here!" Francisco knew too.

José pushed open the car door, his pulse pounding blood through his ears.

"What are you doing?" Francisco yelled. *"Let's go."*

There José sat with a man in a pink shirt telling him to run, run from whatever it was he did. Did he stay or go? Would he run over whatever it was he hit if he did? What was right? For him? For . . . whatever it was? He felt the sweat pool on his scalp, his entire life before him, all his hopes and dreams.

Francisco took him by the chin. *"Listen to me. I'm your friend. I'm your manager. The only way to get out of this is to go!"*

That settled it. Francisco knew too. Even sitting there in the carport with Nina, José wondered if Francisco saw it all. José wondered how Francisco knew that if he wanted to save his career, his life, he'd have to put the car in drive and drive away.

"*Let's get out of here. Now, José!*"

But José scrambled out of the car.

"*I can't.*"

He saw her, the child.

"Nina, standing in the middle of the street, looking down at her little body, I felt a terror like I'd never known in my life.

"People began to gather, and the mother rushed at me, hitting me with her fists and crying out, her sobs so loud and long as if she wanted God to hear, and I tried to calm her, me the killer of her child. I can still remember her crying and screaming for God to give her daughter back."

Nina's eyes were filling with tears.

"I saw the mother standing in the street, looking down at her dead child." He rested his forehead in the palm of his hand. He didn't want to see the expression on Nina's face. He didn't even know why he wanted to bring her here. "I live with it every day, Nina."

Nina rested a hand on his shoulder, her touch firm and comforting. He sank himself into the feeling for just a moment, then turned to face her.

"I was convicted of involuntary manslaughter. A law

called criminally negligent homicide. I was not careful looking at the road and was driving too fast. Manny was there all the time with me."

"What about her family?"

"She was a single mother. They took four years of my life, but I took everything she had."

"How is she doing now?"

"I tried to meet with her several times, but she refused. I go back and put flowers on her daughter's grave and I ask God for answers to why this happened, and I want to see the woman, but I know all she sees in me is the one who killed her little baby."

"It was an accident."

Such a simple statement and one everybody offered. But he heard those words and saw a pair of shoes and a lot of pride. "Doesn't matter now, Nina. It doesn't matter. I can go to Lucinda's grave every day from now until the end of time, and what matters is that I took her life."

So that was it. This was the story nobody knew. It was much worse than they all suspected. Nina felt her heart sink in upon itself with grief; she wanted to fold José into her arms, but there he sat, pressed against his seat, looking as though his memories formed a shell, clear and hard, around him. Eyes glazed, he stared at the steering wheel.

The door to the carport slammed open, and she started as a young man who, quite frankly, put José to shame in the clothing department rushed in and, eschewing the door, jumped into the backseat of the car. "Qué paso, José? And Nina? All right! I missed you the last time I went to the restaurant."

Nina wanted to kiss his sweet cheeks. His enthusiasm touched her right then, down in a place where she'd stored the excitement she once felt about living.

"You guys ready to meet the love of my life?"

José turned to his younger brother, craning his neck back. "Is this the real thing?"

"I think it is, hermano." He sat back, smug and adorable, long lashes curling up as he blinked. "I'm going to marry her."

She'd always wanted a little brother, and this guy would be perfect.

"How long have you guys been together?" she asked.

Eduardo grinned and cocked his head to the side. "A week."

Nina turned around, trying not to laugh.

But the silence returned as Eduardo saw his brother's face and gave credence to the importance of the car in which they sat. He put his hand on his brother's shoulder and squeezed. "They want you in the kitchen, hermano."

"All right," said José.

Good, thought Nina. *Get him out of this place.*

Eduardo hopped out of the car, leaving a smidge of his good cheer behind.

"I promised you a bath," José said.

She smiled and nodded. "Thanks."

He replaced the tarp, locked up the carport, and ushered her into the house through the kitchen. Something sizzled on the stove top, and Manuel was busy stirring up something or other. Nina couldn't tell what it was. A darker-skinned woman holding the solid features of a Mexican native, Juanita, rolled tortillas at the work island. Nina could tell she wasn't Manuel's wife, José's mother, when she failed to hug José but just gave him a shy smile as Eduardo introduced her. "Nina, this is Juanita."

José introduced her to his mother, Maria, who was busy setting the table in the dining room. First she drew him into a warm embrace. José melted a little, wilting just slightly in the embrace of his mother.

Then she hugged Nina and welcomed her. Nina looked into the eyes of this woman and saw something she'd never seen before, a love that wishes for the best, even when that best is difficult.

Oh my.

She caught her breath.

José informed her of Nina's wish for a bath, and a minute later Maria led Nina up the stairs. Maria, with pleasant, open features spread serenely across her face, was one of the prettiest women Nina had ever seen. Plump and soft, she wore her childbearing and her years of living with Manuel with honor and a sense of accomplishment. Her hair, pulled back into a tight bun at the nape of her neck, held very little gray, and she wore almost no makeup.

This is what women should strive for, Nina thought. *This is beauty far deeper than the skin, beauty that mirrors the heart.* She thought of her own mother, then frowned.

"It's good to see you again."

"Yes," Nina nodded as they made for the top of the steps.

"So the two of you took the day off?"

"I was . . . kind of fired today."

Maria nodded. "Yeah . . . I heard. I didn't want to mention it if you didn't want to bring it up. I spoke to Manny. I'm sorry. You shouldn't take it personally, though." She rested her hand on the newel post. "Do you need to borrow any clothes? Because you could try some of mine." She chuckled.

Nina held up her backpack. "Thank you. But I have everything I need right in here. I just have to freshen up a bit."

Freshen up a bit? Nina wanted to laugh at her own formality, for despite their warmth, these were what her mother would have called "classy people."

"Right in here. Would you like me to run the water for you?"

"No, thank you. I think I can do it myself."

When Maria left the bathroom, the door clicked quietly, a homey sound. Nina wanted to cry she felt so cared for.

"This is silly," she whispered. "It's only a bath."

The towels sat warm and soft in her hands, and she raised them to her face, breathing in the fresh, clean scent, a beach scent, a decidedly noncity scent.

José is a genius, she thought, wondering how he knew exactly what she needed.

From the living room, José watched the scene in the kitchen and wondered why he stayed away from here. What was wrong with him? Had the heat of the kitchen taken away his common sense?

One of Juanita's large tortillas sizzled on the griddle; Eduardo hovered over the preparations like the Suvirans had invited royalty over for dinner. Eduardo clapped his father on the back, his words tumbling over each other. *"Smells good! How's it coming, old man?"* He rubbed his hands together.

"When I'm finished, that chicken will taste like caviar." Manuel adjusted the flame.

José loved the bravado of his family.

Eduardo tasted the sauce in a bowl on the countertop,

looking much like his brother Manny. *"It has to be perfect."* He turned to Juanita, who was kneading more flour. *"That's it, Juanita! You show it who's boss."* And he mimicked her movements, his infectious excitement drawing a smile out of the cook. He clapped his hands—"Okay! Okay!"—and tasted a flauta from a dish at the end of the counter. "Okay! Está bien! Wow!"

José felt like he was watching a dance. What he wouldn't give to be innocent like Eduardo once again. To think a woman would want to go out with him, to get to know him, all of him, because there was nothing to hide, nothing to be so ashamed of that the relationship would never make it past it.

Eduardo picked up a dish of three-colored rice arranged in stripes of red, white, and green. *"You outdid yourself! It's the Mexican flag!"*

He was a good boy. Not much promise like his older brothers, José knew. But then again, not as much opportunity to make grave, unforgivable mistakes either. When Eduardo finished college, he'd make a good bank manager or stockbroker. He liked numbers.

Manuel grabbed a chile roasting over an open flame on the stove. José stared at the flame, then took the bandage off his hand. He examined the seared skin of his palm and tucked the bandage in his pocket.

Seventeen

Maria laid a hand on her son's shoulder. How does one watch her child leave this earth before his death, exchanging his life and vitality for sorrow and penance?

She watched her son Eduardo in the kitchen and remembered when this one, José, the one who opened her womb, ran around their home in Mexico, shouting at the top of his lungs and singing all the time. José alone would come sit beside her and tell her he loved her without her having to say it first. José knew when she was upset about something. He had always lain down on the bed next to her, saying little, just lending his presence.

Was it any wonder he'd befriended this pregnant girl, Nina? Maria could picture the day they'd had together so far. Small conversations hanging along a cord of silence. José felt comfortable in silence, even in the happy days. But this Nina? What would she think of her son, so quiet, so sober? Maria would have given anything to see José like he used to be.

She fingered the gold bracelet surrounding her wrist, a gift from him after signing his very first professional contract with Club Madrid.

Something was burning inside of him, something she doubted he could name. She was beyond trying anymore, and sometimes she wanted to shock him out of this state. *"You want to tell me what's going on?"*

He flexed his hand. Maria noticed the burn but said nothing. She'd put that in God's hands awhile ago.

She squeezed his shoulder and sighed. *"Your brother called and said you left without a word, chasing after this girl, Nina."*

José said nothing.

She wished he would speak, and like her own mother would have, she filled in the silence. *"Then you just show up here with her. Manny is very disappointed, José. I've never seen him like this before. And he's right. What were you thinking, abandoning your brother? You're the main chef."*

José looked up. Finally. *"I know I messed up, but Manny fired Nina."*

"So what? That doesn't justify your behavior. Now, Manny tells me that she's pregnant. What do you have to do with that?"

That was it, wasn't it? Dear God, here she thought he was in pain and he and this Nina girl—*"Look at me!"*

He shook his head.

"And they tell me you were in the car? With Nina?"

She watched with sadness and hope as his face broke into a thousand pieces.

"What is it, Son? What's wrong? I don't want to see you like before."

Although he was still a man of sorrows, it was true José had at least ventured into a breathing space he hadn't been in since the accident. And nothing would jeopardize that. She would do her best to make sure of it.

Exhaustion settled like sea spray on José, seeping into the marrow of his bones. Traveling all over the city, on high alert with a pregnant woman, a woman carrying a child inside her, a child he wanted to save in hopes of what? To finally atone?

But could that be?

He thought of Lucinda and saw the butterfly in the street, its wings sticking in the stream of blood that flowed from the child. He thought of Celia, Lucinda's mother, and wondered did she ever have another child? Where was she today? Eating dinner with her family at the beach? José had no idea. Perhaps she was sitting alone, looking at a little snapshot, or working hard at the shoe store.

He sobbed.

The cry came out of him before he could stop it. But the touch of his mother's hand, her beautiful face, the way, well, she just knew. She knew he was a wreck inside, she knew he was mutilating himself, but she trusted him somehow to get through it. She had faith in him.

And being here, in this house, being home. It was too much.

She leaned over and put her arms around him as he sobbed, allowing something to release in him he never had before, something that watered the dried-up belief that he deserved to live a life that meant something, anything.

"Cry it all out," she whispered, as if that were possible. He wrapped his arms around her waist from where he sat and rested his bristled cheek against her bosom.

Nina felt like she was fifteen again, listening to some boy's mother yell at him about her. Last time it was Jason Campbell and he'd been comforting Nina down in his basement. Really. It was the third anniversary of her father's death, and she'd become good friends with Jason, a transfer student, that year. Mrs. Campbell practically pulled him by his ear up the steps to the kitchen and proceeded to accuse them of everything Nina, at that time, hadn't begun to experience. Boy, would Mrs. Campbell have a fit now!

But Maria Suviran was doing a good enough job on her own.

Nina raised her hands to her face and slid beneath the surface of the water. José didn't deserve this.

And this baby.

She wept, shame mixing with her tears, her heart breaking for the first time since she was twelve years old.

José pulled away from his mother and kissed her on the cheek. "I'd better go check on Nina."

Maria nodded.

"*And, Mama, the baby is not mine. You knew that, didn't you?*"

She spread her lips in a tight, sad smile. "*I know. I'm sorry I doubted you.*"

"*I haven't been with a woman in a long, long time. I don't know if—*"

His mother stopped his words, putting two fingers against his lips. "*Do not guess what your future holds, José. You can't second-guess these matters.*"

He found Nina in his old bedroom where she had laid out her clothes. Dressed in his mother's white robe, she held a framed picture. Eight years old he was that day, kicking around a soccer ball.

"You were cute," she said. "A cute little boy."

"Thank you."

"I need to get dressed now."

He backed out of the room.

Maria, having set the water glasses around the dining room table, entered the kitchen. Steam was rising from pots on the stove. She lifted the lid off a pot of rice. Yes, just as it should be. Then added a little cilantro to the platter of chicken Manuel had made. She lifted it up. *"Look how beautiful!"*

Eduardo hurried into the kitchen. "She's here!" He kissed his mother. "Everything's ready, right?"

"Ready. What's her name?"

"Veronica."

Maria laughed as her youngest walked around the kitchen making sure everybody knew how to pronounce his girlfriend's name. Of course, he was pronouncing it "Beronica," but she didn't have the heart to tell him. Maria had picked up English more readily than the rest of her family, having studied it at the university she attended before meeting Manuel, her tongue easily finding the American pronunciation of most words, her accent lilting and soft.

Eduardo ran out the front door to welcome his ladylove. Maria knew better than to think, with Eduardo, that this Veronica was really the one.

Let him dream a little, hope a little, look some more, she thought. He was young and able to fall in love at a moment's notice. Just as it should be.

Salsa music began in the living room, and Maria heard the slide of Eduardo's feet on the wooden floor. Eduardo was an even better dancer than José, not that she would have admitted that to José. At least she wouldn't have years before. José probably wouldn't care these days.

Eduardo sang with the music, off-key. Well, José could sing better than his brother, and Manny, he could sing better than every single one of them.

So? Eduardo dances first and then introduces the family later? Well, there could be worse things. She shrugged, made for the door to the dining room, and watched a little from the side as Eduardo, hips swaying, danced toward Veronica.

Yes, the lovely Veronica. Her dark, chestnut hair hung in glossy waves and her pink spring dress seemed festive, yet respectful. This must be serious, because, truthfully, some of the girls Eduardo brought home . . . Maria shuddered at the thought of their bellies peeking above the low waistbands of their shrink-wrapped jeans. Had they no self-respect? Where were their mothers when they needed clothing advice, eh?

Eduardo took Veronica into his arms and they danced together, hesitantly, yet something undeniable was there. Perhaps . . . no. Not yet. Eduardo had too much charm, and it needed expending before he'd settle down.

Time for the show.

"Turn that music down!" she said.

Manuel entered behind her, hands untying his apron behind his back, eyes glittering at the music. The boys received their love of dancing from him.

"But wait! The party is just starting," he said.

He took Maria into his arms and she moved into him. Times like this she remembered how much she loved him.

"Well, this is getting good," her husband said in her ear.

She gave him a squeeze and then, out of the corner of her eye, she spotted them, José and a fresh Nina, her blouse replaced by a black tank top. She had pretty arms, lithe and graceful.

Her hair was still damp.

"José! Nina!" Eduardo held out a hand. "You want to dance?"

José hated dancing these days, but here she was, a dancer, and he knew—she blushed and shook her head.

Good.

Maria clapped her hands. *"Okay, enough! It's time to eat."*

"Where are you going? I have the final word here," Manuel protested. As Maria walked away, he repeated it to the boys and to Nina and Veronica as if they understood. *"I always get the last word here, and the last word is . . ."*

She clipped over to the stereo and shut off the music.

He bowed. *"Whatever you say, my queen."*

He opened his arms. *"Sit down everyone."*

Eduardo seated Veronica, pulling out a carved wooden chair. "José, Nina . . . Veronica Suviran, mi novia y futura esposa."

"Nice to meet you," said José.

Veronica gave a little wave of her hand. "Veronica *Kustala*. Nice to meet you."

Nina nodded. "You too."

Veronica turned to Eduardo. "Novia?"

Eduardo grinned. *"Novia* means 'girlfriend.' *Futura esposa* means . . . 'future wife.'"

Veronica flipped her hair back over her shoulder. "Eduardo es loco. He's trying to teach me Spanish."

Eduardo turned around and pulled a bottle of tequila and some port glasses from a cabinet. "Nina! Qué? Un tequilita?"

"No . . ." Nina hesitated.

Of course, the child, thought José.

Eduardo filled her glass anyway. "No, no, no . . . family custom, yes?"

"Eduardo . . . ," Maria began.

"José?" he asked.

"No, gracias."

"Come on, hermano." Eduardo would not be put off. "Mommy? Veronica?"

He poured the tequila into their glasses.

Manuel put his glass forward. *"Hey, respect the gray hair."*

"Oh yeah. Sorry." Eduardo tipped some tequila into his father's glass, then sat down.

"Shall we say grace?" Maria said, folding her hands.

Eduardo reddened. "Say grace before the toast?"

José laid his napkin in his lap. Maybe someday Eduardo wouldn't be embarrassed. But today was not that day. And José understood what that felt like too.

Manuel began, *"In the name of the Father . . ."*

"Eh, Papi," Eduardo interrupted, and José felt that older-brother impatience rising in his throat. Would the boy stop interfering, micromanaging, making everything such a big to-do? "Veronica and I are going to say grace." He turned to Veronica. "Ready? You repeat after me."

Her brows raised in surprise, but she pressed her hands together in front of her chest. Poor thing, only a week of Spanish lessons and already Eduardo was putting her on the spot.

In Spanish, Eduardo began the prayer. *"The One . . ."*

"The One . . . ," they all repeated.

"Papi, this is for Veronica. Thank you." He looked at Veronica. "Sorry."

And Veronica repeated each phrase after Eduardo. Her Spanish was ill pronounced and full of the wrong inflection, but José took it for the gift it was, for what she was willing to learn, not realizing she was speaking a children's prayer that rhymes in Spanish.

"The One . . . that gave us our life . . . Bless . . . this food . . . Amen!"

"Amen!" they all said.

"Muy bien!" Eduardo grabbed Veronica's hand. "Great job!"

José crossed himself, as did Maria and Manuel. Nina tried but failed, sort of waving her hand in a circle in front of her chest. José thought it was beautiful.

These poor young women, subjected to the Suviran men.

A sense of gratitude filled him.

Eduardo said, "Bien, bien. Salud, ahora. Now, we can toast, no?"

"Salud!"

They raised their glasses together. Nina took a tiny sip and looked at José. Was she rethinking the plans she'd already started making about the baby? He couldn't be sure, but he felt hopeful.

Manuel turned to Nina and said in English, "Nina, you like osteones?"

Eduardo laughed. "That was good, Dad! Wow! Muy bien . . . That was good, Dad." To the girls, "*Osteones* means 'oysters.'"

Of all of them, Manuel's refusal to learn English embarrassed Eduardo the most. José shook his head. Well, at least

Eduardo was trying positive reinforcement, but José knew his father, and he wouldn't give up without more of a fight that this!

"I love oysters," said Nina.

Eduardo reached for a bowl and handed it to Veronica. "One time I dove into this river on our ranch in Mexico."

"How I miss that ranch!" said Manuel.

José clenched his fist. They'd given up so much for his career.

Eduardo was on a roll, however. He loved to spin a story, and this he did while they passed around the bowls and platters and filled up their plates. "When I dove in, my legs were sticking out of the water and my whole head was stuck in mud. I found out the river was only three feet deep." He nodded, earnest. "Manny had to come to my rescue and pull me out by the legs. When he pulled me out, an oyster shell cut my arm." He pulled up the sleeve on his shirt to expose a thick white snake of a scar that traveled from his wrist to his elbow. "Seventy-seven stitches. If I would have moved my arm inches to the right, this scar would have been on my face. And beautiful Veronica wouldn't be here."

"Why wouldn't I be here?" she said.

"Because . . . I wouldn't be as handsome."

Laughter rose up to bounce off the ceiling, descending back down upon them.

Manuel turned to Maria. *"At this pace, I'll never be a grandfather."*

Eduardo seemed bent on controlling the conversation. José knew there wasn't much he could do about it, so he relaxed and ate his family's good cooking.

"Anyways, Nina," Eduardo said. "I heard Manny fired you because you were late."

"Eduardo," José said. So much for relaxing.

"And you!" Eduardo pointed at José. "You walked out on him today?"

Manuel turned to Maria. *"What's he talking about?"*

"How Manny fired the girl."

Manuel's voice dropped and he focused on his youngest son. *"Don't start . . ."*

But Eduardo was still in charge of the show. "He fired me too! Before I even started working."

Maria wiped her mouth. "You never showed up to work."

Eduardo waved a hand. "Manny needs to learn how to cook anyway. He's too busy cracking the whip like El Jeneral . . . El Jeneral . . . up on his fine horse . . . There should be a statue of him up in front of the restaurant!"

Maria shot him a warning look. "You should take Manny as an example. He's worked hard all his life. He started from zero and look where he is now . . . unlike you."

Now, maybe that would put the little man in his place. José didn't dare to break into the grin he felt.

The food and the wine did their job as everyone ate the sizzling oysters and rice and fresh salads of mango and avocado and jicama. And José felt a pride in being a part of this family, these people gathered around. True, they were no longer in their homeland, but they were connected to it enough to bring pieces of it along.

Maria set down her fork and dabbed at her lips with a napkin. "I normally don't share this, but in the early years of our marriage we couldn't have children. We tried . . . we tried hard. We tried everything, but—"

"Mama," Eduardo broke in as expected. "Don't mention such things in front of the children."

José's heart hurt for him a little as the joke fell flat, and in front of the fair Veronica.

Maria continued. "And then, when we were about to give up, one of Manuel's cousins back in Puerto Rico, a social worker, called us, and before we knew it, we had adopted this beautiful baby. He was not even three years old . . . a really precious boy." She smiled at Nina, her eyes locking into the gaze of the young woman. "I think the only difference between my three sons is the way Manny came to us."

Nina looked at José as if to ask if he'd planned this.

No. No, he did not.

But he would have if he had that kind of power. And he had a feeling his mother would speak the words he could not.

Nina walked around the perimeter of the room, mouth open. She'd never guessed this about José. How did he keep this from the staff? And Manny? Obviously the man could keep a secret as well.

Nina had never seen so much soccer paraphernalia gathered in one place. Framed photos inched out almost all the wall space in Manuel's study; they served as a time-line of José's career from boyhood teams all the way up to pro. And trophies, and ribbons, and plaques. Almost too many to count. Now, she didn't have this many trophies in her room at home, but she was no sloucher in the dance competitions. She had done all right.

Truth was, she barely recognized José in those shots. Truth also was, if it had been *that* José who cooked in the kitchen at El Callejon, she'd have gone after him well before Pieter. No beard. A visible confidence exuding in every shot.

She hugged her arms and had to chuckle. What was she thinking? A professional soccer player interested in the daughter of a school uniform salesman from Philadelphia?

Even now, bushy bearded and haunted, José had no eyes for her whatsoever. She didn't need the complication in her life to be sure, but it would have been nice to think he at least found her attractive.

Like she needed that kind of baggage right now along with her own two-ton suitcase. No thanks.

Still, the exhilaration on José's face as he was captured midkick by a photographer brought a smile to Nina's lips. She'd like to see him look like that again, and in that moment, she somewhat understood the sadness his parents must have felt at the change in the son they loved so much.

Perhaps there wouldn't be a return to that carefree José of years ago, but couldn't someone help him break free from his chains?

Nina felt for Lucinda's mother, but the fact remained, she'd let her three-year-old daughter out of her sight. Yes, José was partly to blame, and yes, a mother will make mistakes, some with ramifications to last a lifetime. But a mother was always responsible for her flesh and blood.

Nina realized her hands were pressed protectively across her abdomen.

Manuel walked into the room.

He pointed to the picture Nina was looking at. *"This is Francisco. He used to be José's manager when he played fútbol."*

"Soccer?" Nina asked, clueing herself in to the word *fútbol*.

"Soccer, sí. You like soccer?"

"I don't play soccer. Do you play?"

"Sure I do. Every Thursday and Saturday. They call me the old man, but I can keep up with all the kids."

Now, that one Nina couldn't translate at all, so she just grinned that didn't-understand-a-word-but-I'm-smiling-because-I-like-you-and-don't-wish-to-offend-you smile. He pointed to another picture, apparently not offended.

"José—that was his professional debut."

"I'm sorry." That one she could figure out.

Manuel sat down on a leather chair. *"He never played again after the accident. No more soccer. Sit."*

He held out a hand, and Nina sat beside him on a matching seat. *"The accident cost him his passion, and without it you can't play soccer."*

Nina only understood a few words: "soccer," "accidente," and "passion." Add two and two together and she could figure it out.

Maria entered the room and sat on the arm of her husband's chair. Nina couldn't imagine such an intimate relationship. If she felt that way about Pieter, there'd be no decision to make. She'd be an idiot not to have the baby.

Maria took her husband's hand. "He's saying you can't play soccer without passion." She smiled at Manuel. "This man never wanted to learn English in his whole life, have you?"

"Noooo . . ."

Nina nodded. "I understand what he's saying."

Maria said, "He understands a lot more than you think." She caressed him with her gaze. "Don't you?"

"What are you saying?"

"You don't like to speak English, but you understand everything."

"My family speaks Spanish." He shrugged. *"If you want to speak to me, speak Spanish."* He smiled; clearly he was speaking tongue in cheek.

Nina stood up. "Well, it's getting late. I need to get back to the city."

Manuel said, *"No, you, José, stay here."*

"You see how he speaks English?" Maria said. "He doesn't because he's lazy! But he's right. You should stay here and rest."

"Thank you, but I really can't."

Manuel nodded. *"It's been a pleasure. This is your home."* He stood up and kissed Nina on the cheek. Tears filled her eyes. She knew he meant what he said.

"Gracias," she said.

"Take care." Maria hugged her, a warm, mother's hug.

Eighteen

Eduardo and Veronica were staring at each other on the couch when Nina walked into the room.

"Are you looking for José?" Eduardo asked, refusing to remove his gaze from Veronica.

"Yes."

"In the carport."

"Thank you."

She headed through the kitchen where Juanita loaded up the dishwasher. Juanita smiled and nodded, and Nina wondered how long she'd been working for the Suvirans.

Out the back door, past the wheelbarrow and gardening tools, Nina already felt at home, as if this was something she'd been waiting for. She was smart enough to realize everyone felt that way entering this home, but the biggest question remained as to why Manny and José ever wanted to leave it.

Eduardo was smarter than they were giving him credit for, obviously.

She remembered talking with her dad one day about leaving home, asking him why children, if they loved their fathers as much she loved hers, ever left home?

"Because good parents teach their children how to stand on their own two feet, and they tell their children they love them so much and prove it, the children know no matter how far they wander, they will always have a place to come back to, a place to be loved and accepted."

She'd hugged him then and said, "I'm never going to leave you anyway, even if you are a good father."

And she never did. His death made sure of that.

She stepped into the carport.

José leaned against the hood of the old car and stared at the beat-up soccer ball. That little boy, David, never got it back. *So much for my promises.*

And yet. He'd eaten with his family, spent the day with Nina, even stood up to Manny not just for his own sake but for the sake of the entire kitchen staff.

That wasn't so bad, was it? That was something, yes?

It seemed a little crazy, perhaps. But his grandmother

used to tell him, quoting her favorite person, Mother Teresa, "It's not that we must do great things, but that we do small things with great love."

Nina's shadow fell across the cement floor, the sinking sun low behind her. He couldn't see her face against the golden backlight, but he could hear her voice. "I need to go home."

He just couldn't bring himself to end the day. His vision caught two lanterns his father made for walking the beach. "Let's go to the beach and then we can go from there."

He tossed Nina the ball, and in that motion, he felt like he was letting something go. Yes, Nina needed a friend, but he needed to trust her too. Maybe he needed a friend even more than she did. Heaven knew he'd been alone for so long.

"Sure," she said.

A few minutes later, carrying lanterns that looked like illuminated boxes, one white, one red, they made their way into the grapy dusk.

Nina held up her lantern. "I never saw anything like this before."

"My father made them. They say he has too much time on his hands. But after he sold the ranch"—José shrugged— "he needed something to do, and Mama wanted him out of her way around the house."

"I just adore him. He is so great. Is he from Mexico?"

The wind blew over them as they stepped onto the creamy sand.

"No. My father's from Puerto Rico and my mother's from Mexico. So I'm . . . eh . . . RicoMex."

She laughed.

"It means half Puerto Rican, half Mexican."

"It's all the same to me."

José realized he knew so little about her. Obviously not Hispanic, what type of family did she come from? Irish? German? Or had they been over here so long they were simply typical Americans with nothing left of their old countries in them?

He always thought that was sad.

She took off her sandals and scooped them up to dangle from her fingers. "So, is it always like that? I mean, did you grow up with . . . that?"

"What?"

"Joy? Love?"

Her description of his family made him smile. "That's nothing. I mean, when my whole family gets together, it's really amazing! The talking, the food, the music, the dancing—salsa, meringue—wow. It's beautiful."

"I'll bet it is." Her voice lowered, fraying around the edges into something softer, maybe, he thought, filled with a little hope. "How does Manny feel about people knowing he's adopted?"

"To us that doesn't make a difference."

"You're *seriously* lucky. You have a good family."

"Yeah. What about your family?"

"My dad passed away when I was twelve. No brothers or sisters. So that's my family." She rubbed her arms.

"Here." José took off his chef's jacket and put it around her shoulders.

"Thank you."

They continued down the beach, gulls circling overhead, the sun below the western horizon now.

"What about your mom?" he asked.

"After Dad died, she just kind of sat on the couch with the remote and never moved on. I raised myself . . . and her." She pulled the jacket tightly around her. "I'm tired of always having to deal with something, José. Just once, I wanted something to work the way I planned it. Just once."

"How was it dealing with your dad's death?"

"I don't know. It's hard for me to remember what the twelve-year-old me was feeling. I think that my mom took it so hard, I didn't get the chance to grieve in a healthy way. It was like I had to take care of her, you know? At first, it brought us closer together, but I eventually turned into the typical teenager and all that grief turned into resentment."

"One night I got stoned out of my mind and went home. I walked into her room, and there she was, watching TV. I looked at her and started laughing at her, pointing right in her face. She just sat there, taking it all without a word, and I started to cry."

Nina wiped the mist from her eyes, her voice beginning to shake. "I told her how much I missed my dad too; I knew she was in pain, but I was in pain too." Tears rolled down her cheeks. "It was like, for the first time, she saw me again. She stood up and hugged me." She paused, gathered herself, and said, "Then I got the munchies." She exhaled a laugh. "We ate some doughnuts and talked about him all night. The next morning I woke up and felt like I had a mom again. But . . . it was too late."

They sat down together on the sand. Nina leaned back on her hands. José, feeling the fatigue of the day and realizing that tomorrow, knowing Manny, would be even more exhausting, lay down beside her. He handed her a seashell.

"When I was about eighteen," she continued, "my mom held out her hand and waved her wedding ring at me—this tiny stone my dad probably got at a pawn shop."

Nina wiggled her fingers like she was showing off an engagement ring. "She said, 'You need to get you one of these.'" She looked down on her hand, so devoid of a wedding ring. José had never seen something so stark. "She loved him so much she never took that ring off. That's what I want, José. I want to bring a child into this world out of love, with a man who's gonna take care of us. I don't have that. I can't have this baby and watch it suffer with me. Now *you'd* make a great father, José. You just need to meet a little number like your brother Eduardo has. First you need a little cleanup, though. What's with the beard?"

José rolled his eyes. "We're talking about you, Nina. You're not being fair to yourself. You'd make a great mother."

"Yeah, I had such a stellar example." She picked at her skirt. "Someday . . . not now."

She stared at the waves. "You know . . . what I'm carrying inside me is not that little girl. It's not that little girl to be reborn."

"I know," he whispered.

"I don't know what I'm doing." She wiped her eyes. "I'm gonna need a friend next week."

Helplessness covered José completely. So he said nothing as she sniffed back the tears, hoping that being there was enough for now.

He put an arm around her and gathered her to his side.

The sun had set hours before, and the chill of the spring evening settled in her bones, the gentle pounding of the surf caressing her ears freely, because the surf would continue to come and come and come, and she didn't have to do a thing but enjoy it. Beside her, José breathed deeply in sleep. She didn't want to go back to the city, not yet. The city would always be there. But today had been special. She snuggled up close to him and closed her eyes there against his warmth. He was a mystery, but he knew how to love in a way that went beyond sex and the gooey feelings of a romance book. She hadn't felt love like this since the day her father left for work and never came home.

Maybe it was time to move beyond that.

The truth of it hit her.

Maybe this baby was a chance to do something right for a change. To stop looking for her dad and become like him instead. Not perfect, but someone who tried to do the right thing.

"But I'm not ready to be a mom," she whispered to the waves.

Just be for now, the waves whispered back.

It did seem as if the new morning held more promise than the old one. But the waves were gone and the only rhythm she heard was that of the train clacking along the tracks back to the city. They'd caught the first train in.

José leaned in. "Look at us. In English you say we are fish out of water, eh?"

"Yes." They couldn't have been more disheveled, and try as they might, they couldn't quite get all the sand out of their clothing and shoes. And José's chef jacket and her loud waitress uniform did nothing to normalize them along the lines of their fellow travelers. Well, it was the early train. Most of them were probably too sleepy to really care.

But she was tired and laid her head on José's shoulder. She slept a little more.

Wide awake, José watched the scenery zip by his window. Nina breathed heavily, and when he looked down at her, he experienced a compassion like he'd never felt before and he understood something. He understood how his family felt when he was in trouble all those years ago, how much they yearned to make things right, to do what they could.

In a way, his failure to move on informed them their affection, their caring, was wasted on him.

Lucinda's not coming back, he thought. *But I can live my life, do something good for a change, and honor her death that way. Anything else would be a waste.*

An idea came to mind.

Would Nina go for it? He doubted it, but maybe he'd convince her.

He looked over at Nina, her dark lashes soft crescents against her pale cheeks. She'd create a beautiful baby, he realized.

The train pulled into Penn Station as the dawn grayed the sky. He nudged her. "We're here."

José took her hand and they stepped off the train, up the stairs, and onto the streets of the city near Nina's apartment.

She pointed the way, and he accompanied her as the city awakened to another typical day, another turn of the living clock, another dance of people leading and being led, and somehow, despite all the heartache, they all went on, not so much because they had to, but because there was nothing else imaginable. So much possibility, so little creativity, considering.

As they waited for the Walk signal, Nina reached into her bag and pulled out the scarf she'd purchased the day before. She pressed it into his hand. "Here, I want you to keep it." In a way, she looked like a medieval princess handing off her handkerchief to the winner of the tournament. José was no knight in shining armor, he realized, but he hoped he had treated her in kind, with dignity and respect.

"Oh. Thank you."

She laid a hand on his arm and squeezed. Her eyes seemed to say, *Look at me, please*. "You're gonna come with me to the appointment, right?"

José didn't know what to say. How could he go someplace with her where he thought . . . and yet, she was his friend.

She removed her hand, shaking her head. "You know what—don't worry about it. I'll be fine."

"I'll call you." He looked into her eyes. "I'll call you, okay?" And he reached out.

Nina felt connected to him in that embrace. She knew José meant what he said, that truly, for the first time in many years, somebody was willing to actually put himself out for her. It felt strange, and she wasn't sure what to think about being the scrappy person she'd become. But she remembered the waves telling her to be and she heard one more message in the whizzing of the cabs and buses: wait.

Okay then. But not too long. Time is not on my side.

They parted ways. Nina turned toward her building, José back to the station.

Nina stopped in at the drugstore, bought a soda, and made small talk with Carla, who, she found out, had two kids. Her husband worked down at the docks, and she worked this job to put them in the nearby parochial school.

"That's nice," Nina said.

"Oh, you'll do anything for your kids to give 'em a fighting chance," she said.

Nina was thankful she was discreet enough to not mention the test kit she'd bought yesterday.

Only yesterday? It didn't seem possible.

So Nina headed up the steps to her apartment. She put on a little Nina Simone, threw on sweats and a T-shirt, and picked up her book. The weekend sat before her, lonely and filled with a whole lotta nothin'. But Monday she'd call Frannie at the new restaurant, and she'd be working soon enough.

She figured Frannie would be just as difficult as Manny, but she was doing a good turn for her friend, José, and maybe that would make all the difference.

Maybe she'd call home. Maybe some relationships were worth the bearing of the burden. She only had one mother, and sure, she was far from perfect, but did she deserve to lose a daughter because she couldn't move beyond losing the love of her life?

The answer to that didn't matter. Nina decided to wait, however, until after the baby situation was behind her.

Nineteen

José approached El Callejon as Manny was unlocking the door. He couldn't wait to run his plan by Manny and see what he thought. Manny, of all people, would understand the importance of it.

Manny pushed open the door without a word. A new, stainless-steel pot caught the early morning sun. He motioned for José to enter. He held up the shiny pot and handed it to his brother.

He straightened himself and looked around.

José loved his brother. He loved that Manny couldn't apologize with his mouth but never failed to try to make amends when he went too far. José raised the pot, nodded.

Apology accepted.

They began their usual routine, no mention of the previous day's firing, no mention of the harsh words, the accusations. They were brothers, and José knew that with Manny sometimes words could be taken back. They had to be.

He set a pan to heat on the stove, to make a little breakfast for himself and Manny. He scrambled eggs, then cooked tomatoes, onions, and chiles down to a concentrated sauce and spooned them over the eggs. Some sliced avocado, and yes, this was good.

Manny offered him a pot; José offered food.

Manny stepped into the work area for just a second. "I talked with my accountant last night. Pepito and the kitchen are getting a raise. We can talk about how much."

José looked up in surprise. "Good." And began chopping onions. Best not to make a big deal about it.

A few minutes later, plates in hand, he entered the bar area where Manny sat drinking a glass of tomato juice, looking over paperwork.

José shoved the paperwork aside and set a plate before Manny, a fork and a napkin. He sat down in front of his own meal, folded his hands, and offered up a prayer, not just of thankfulness, but because of what he had to say to his brother. He crossed himself and picked up his fork, elbowing Manny.

Manny elbowed back.

Then José.

Then Manny.

José snaked back his arm around Manny's shoulders, and Manny reared forward in a fierce hug, drawing his brother to him tightly. He squeezed and then let go.

"Enough!" Manny cleared his throat and they set back to breakfast.

"Let's talk about the Salmon Norteño, the special I want to come up with: asparagus, mushroom, cactus, throw in some avocado, mango—"

José stilled him, holding up a hand. He whispered his idea into his brother's ear.

Manny drew back, eyes wide. "You're gonna do what?"

Twenty

Five and a half years later.

José watched her play on the beach, the surf rolling in with a calm rhythm that day, the sky, streaks of gray with slivers of silver sun, overhead. She skipped in the sand, her bare feet soaking in the cold ocean foam as the water sought the shore over and over again. Always coming, always in the same way.

He'd dressed her that morning in her favorite red skirt that now rippled like a flag in the same wind that reached down and snatched in a twirling grasp her flyaway brown pigtails. The way she concentrated on the seashells, it seemed like she'd forgotten him sitting farther up the shore on the soft sand, but every so often she'd pick up a shell or some driftwood and raise it up for him to see. It had been easy to name her once she arrived. Bella. Beautiful. The entire family rallied around him the day he brought her home from the hospital, clueless and thinking he must have been crazy to have taken all this on his shoulders.

And Nina, she turned away, crying, as he and Bella slid into Manuel's sedan, Maria in the front seat, reaching back to tuck a soft white blanket around the newborn baby girl.

He left the city that day for good, moved back home, and opened up José's Place, a little eatery that specialized in the food he'd learned to make at home. Just a few tables, and the patrons who came again and again learned to expect Bella to be around. More than one person said, "You need to name this place Bella's."

"You're right about that," José would say.

It was a great life, watching her grow, taking Bella to Eduardo's wedding to the fair Veronica when she was three and last year to the opening of Manny's second restaurant. Both uncles adored her, Eduardo always buying fashionable clothing for his niece, something José was grateful for; Manny, having bought her a horse, already planning out her education as well.

And he loved this child. He never knew how much a person could love someone. And even as his purpose was set before him and she filled his loneliness, he understood even more deeply what Celia had lost when Lucinda was killed beneath the wheels of his car.

Which he sold the week after Nina said yes to his proposition: you give this baby life, Nina, and I'll make sure she has a good one from there on out.

He was doing his best to deliver on that promise.

Two other girls joined up with Bella, the small one carrying a big yellow bucket to match her blonde hair, the other, dark curls wiggling in the wind, sporting a billowy, dark blue shirt. They all knelt down to examine shells. José looked at his watch. She would be arriving soon. Bella asked to meet her mother for her fifth birthday, and Nina said she'd show up once she had a break.

José was surprised. They'd agreed it was best for her to get on with her life, for Bella's sake. An in-and-out mother wasn't something either José or Nina wanted for their daughter.

But Bella was insistent.

Everybody in the family tried to explain that this wasn't something that would last, that Nina was part of a traveling production, dancing all over the world in *42nd Street*, "a sparkly, beautiful Broadway show," José told Bella.

So far Bella didn't hold Nina's absence against her, and José promised himself he'd do his best to make sure she never did. But in the end, that was up to Bella.

The parents of the two little girls approached the group gathered by the surf. They seemed to be tourists, not residents who were just snatching a few minutes on the beach before work or school pickup. "Come on, girls!" the mother called.

The father looked up at him, and José knew exactly what he thought, scruffy-bearded guy on the beach, hippie shirt, drawstring pants. He probably wouldn't trust himself either if he didn't know him!

He couldn't help but smile. He'd been threatening to shave off his beard for some time but never seemed to get around to it. They were just too busy, and fatherhood proved to be more than just getting the little one dressed in the morning and a bedtime kiss. No, there was a lot of life to be lived in the in-between.

"Bella!" he called. "Come get your shoes on!"

Nina pulled Bubbles out of her bag as she sat in the cab. She couldn't believe this was really the right thing to do, but José thought it would be all right, and she had learned, if nothing else in the past five years, to trust his judgment.

Maria called her and assured her the family would be waiting with opened arms. But as much as she longed to be folded in the soft arms of José's mother, she only agreed to meet Bella alone, with José.

But she had Bubbles with the blue scarf around its neck to comfort her. She lifted it to her mouth and kissed it, feeling sorry for it still, the poor thing. Red yarn held the arm she'd yanked off years ago back in place. She kissed it again, thankful he had fallen out of her backpack, thankful for Bella, for José, for the way her life had been turned around by the act of growing a baby, of giving birth, of giving someone a chance.

Life changed after that. You give birth, you can do anything! She hit the pavement again, found a studio that let her dance in exchange for whatever they needed. She mopped, answered phones, fetched carryout. It was worth it.

She worked at Frannie's, who, yes, was extremely demanding, but fair, and two years after Bella was born, she was hired for *42nd Street*'s traveling production. She'd been on the road ever since, save holidays and time off, which she spent in Philadelphia with her mother or just driving around the countryside. She gave up her apartment in the city after the show hit the road, and she didn't shed a tear for that ratty old place. In fact, she wondered how she had stood it for so long.

Thank God Bella came along and shook her up.

She'd needed a good shaking up.

And now, she couldn't walk away again. She knew that. When she said yes to Bella's request, she said yes to much more than an hour or two. That frightened her, but as much as José's family could rally around Bella, once she entered her life, there could only be one mother, and Nina was it.

José walked toward the shore. He didn't know why he called for Bella to come get her shoes on. It appeared the love of the beach was genetic, because Bella loved standing by the waves, listening to the surf, digging her toes in the sand as much as Nina did. They'd found themselves on Long Island a great deal during the pregnancy, walking along the sand or just sitting, staring at the surf.

He ran along beside Bella now and she fled, laughing, her pale face full-on in the wind.

He scooped her up and she laughed harder, squealing, "Daddy!"

He buried his face into her neck, shaking his head back and forth. Maria had given her a bath before they came, and she smelled of bubblegum shampoo, rose perfume, and the salty air. It was Bella's smell, and he breathed it in.

They ran some more on the sand, doing cartwheels and looking for that final shell. There it sat. A small conch. Unusual this far north. She picked it up.

"You can always take a piece of the ocean with you," he said as they walked toward the street.

"How?"

"Well, when you take a seashell home, you put it right to your ear and you can hear the ocean. You wanna try it?"

"Sure."

Grabbing her underneath her arms, he scooped her

up and onto the wall separating the beach from the street. "Okay, one . . . two . . . three . . ."

She put the shell to her ear. "I can't hear it, Dad."

He sat down next to her. "Ah, well, you're at the ocean. But when you leave the ocean, then you can hear it."

She held up the shell again. Waited. "I can hear it now!"

He smiled. "You can hear it now, eh?"

He took her foot and twisted on the pink canvas sneaker. Compliments of Eduardo. Aunt Veronica probably had something to do with it as well.

Next foot. Good.

Her little dress blew in the breeze, and he lifted a scarf out of his pocket. A white scarf with sea-blue designs. He figured this was the time to bring out what was once her mother's. Nina would appreciate the gesture. José had most certainly defended her honor.

He tied it around her head. "Wow!" He whistled, just like he did in the bazaar to Nina years before.

"How do I look?" Bella asked.

"You look beautiful." Definitely more beautiful than Helen.

He sat back down next to her. "You sure about this?"

She nodded. "I know it's just for today, Dad. Don't worry."

He barked out a laugh. He couldn't help himself. "Has Grandmother Maria been talking to you?"

"Grandpapa."

"All right, then. Are you scared?"

She nodded.

"Me too." He took her hands. "I used to get very scared right before a game." He patted his stomach. "I'd get butter- flies right here."

Bella laughed. "You had butterflies inside of you?"

"Used to." He ran the backs of his fingers over her wind- blown cheek. "Like big wings flapping inside me. Much less since you were born. You feel like that?"

She nodded. "A little."

"You know what Grandma did for me and Uncle Manny when we got scared?"

Bella opened her mouth in shock. "Uncle Manny gets scared?"

José laughed. "We all get scared sometimes. Even Uncle Manny. Grandma would plug our ears so that nothing bad would get inside our heads. It would keep us safe and the butterflies would go away. She called it 'magic fingers.'"

"Really? Magic?"

"Yes. All moms and dads have them. So. Can I plug your ears?"

"Okay."

He gently closed her ears with his forefingers. "Okay, now shut your eyes."

She did and he counted to ten. "There. Now you plug mine."

He leaned in as she returned the favor, her face sober and hopeful. "All right. Now close your eyes, Dad."

After ten seconds he opened his eyes and shook his head a little. "Ah, much better. You feel it? You feel better?"

She nodded. "Is she going to live with us?"

"I don't know. But I know she's going to be so glad to meet you."

The cab pulled up. This was it.

"Here she comes, Bella. Let's go." He slid off the wall and lifted Bella down.

Nina climbed out of the taxi, her face pale.

José waved, and a smile, that beautiful smile mirrored on the face of his daughter, split her face.

Bella looked at him and he nodded, then she turned back to Nina as she approached. Nina's mouth fell open in awe and she patted the tears away that had spilled onto her cheeks.

Nina knelt down and took Bella's hand. "Do you know who I am?"

"You're my mama."

A sob escaped Nina and she laughed as she cried. Joy mixed in with the tears. She opened her bag and pulled out that teddy bear from years gone by.

"I brought this for you." She held it out.

Bella stared at her, then looked at José. He nodded to tell her it was all right.

She took the bear and brought it close to her chest.

"This was the last gift my father gave to me," Nina said.

"Thank you."

Bella hugged the bear and ran her chin along its head. She handed Nina the shell in return.

"Thank you," Nina said.

"You're welcome. When you're away from the ocean, you can hear the waves. Anytime you want."

Nina looked up at José, and another sob tumbled from her mouth. She stood up and he put his arms around her. "Thank you so much," she cried, her tears soaking into his shirt. "I'm sorry . . ."

"Shh," he said. "We all love you, Nina." And he looked down at Bella, hugging the little bear. Who could have known?

"Bella . . . ," Nina said.

Bella held out her hand. Nina took it.

José scooted around the other side and took Bella's other hand. "Would you like to walk with us?" he asked.

"Yes, I would like that."

They headed toward the surf, waves rolling and crashing, whispering of life, providing a song for the day's dance.

The Film's Production Story

didn't have a big budget, but I had New York City," Monteverde says emphatically. "You can shoot there with 50 million dollars or 1 million dollars and it's still New York City—the biggest celebrity you can find. I needed that city no matter what."

"And he got it," says producer Denise Pinckley, whose feature film credits as production manager include *The Manchurian Candidate*, *The Legend of Bagger Vance*, and *Analyze This*. Pinckley was recommended to Metanoia as a smart producer and a troubleshooter who could make their money go a very long way. At the time, she was considering a job on a big-budget film as a production manager that would also shoot in Manhattan. But her meeting with the charismatic Monteverde made the same dramatic impression that it had made on others. She declined the big Hollywood film and set out to do her best with an indie budget.

"Professionally, it was a choice between something I knew I

could do and something I believed I could do, and *Bella* was where my heart was," says Pinckley. "Alejandro was so committed to *Bella* that once we discussed it, I never wavered in the belief that we could shoot in New York, the way he wanted it, and with the resources we had available."

As the move started to come together, Monteverde also tapped Andrew Cadalago, his good friend from the University of Texas film school, to work as his cinematographer. The two had partnered on student films and had developed a comfortable shorthand for getting the job done artistically and economically.

The next challenge was casting.

"Suddenly, it was three weeks before shooting and we were still seeing actresses," says Verastegui. "I had been wearing the producer's hat for so long, in lots of meetings, that I had forgotten to concentrate on my role as José. Acting is like a muscle and it has to be exercised, so I began to focus on the character."

"In a way, Eduardo is like his character José in real life," explains Monteverde. "I had seen the way he connects with people, and I wanted to capture that. Eduardo is also very handsome but I didn't want the audience to be distracted by that so we came up with the idea of a full beard and long hair. I told him that I didn't want to see anything but his eyes."

"For me, I was eager to erase the last twelve years of my career, the stereotype of the Latin lover," says Verastegi. "José is impulsive on the say of our story, but the thing I like best about him is that he listens. And he is very close to his mother and his family, like I am."

"I know how much Eduardo can communicate with his eyes, and I know that he is a passionate man—but I was very tough on him," admits the director. "Not because he was doing badly, but because I wanted to break him down. I was tougher on him than anyone else on the set. I wanted to break him and capture that vulnerable quality on film."

Looking back on the experience of being directed by his demanding friend, Verastegi says, "Alejandro takes you deep and lets you go, giving the actor the freedom to create. He's my brother."

In the role of Nina, whose wounded spirit touches something deep in José, Monteverde cast actress Tammy Blanchard, who had also recently been hired for Robert DeNiro's big budget feature film production *The Good Shepherd*, opposite Matt Damon. An Emmy-award winner for her star-turning role in ABC's television epic *Me and My Shadows: Life with Judy Garland*. Blanchard was the first actress to read for the role of Nina. Subsequently, she asked her managers to set up a second meeting with the first-time director.

"She said quite directly, 'I want you to know that character is mine.' She was very determined but also very humble. I called her that night and told her that I had faith in her. She had the role."

Blanchard explains, "I don't do a project unless I feel I can put my heart and soul in it. I responded to the brokenness of these people . . . the city of Manhattan is full of people who are lost and confused and everyone is looking for that saving grace to pull them out of their pain. I thought this was a true, honest story."

"Tammy and I would walk around the set talking about the character," Monteverde continues. "And even though she has quite a few emotional scenes, she's a one-taker. If we went further, it's because I had other technical things in mind, but she always got it the first time."

"As soon as we started rehearsing, I could see how talented, and how transparent she was," says Verstegui. "She was full of positive reinforcement and I wanted to protect her with mutual support."

"Nina is a lost lamb and somehow a shepherd comes along," explains Blanchard about her character. "She follows José to a safe place where she can express herself, and when he opens up about his life, he practically breathes life into her."

A third character, a mother who meets José under difficult circumstances at the height of his soccer career, is played by Ali Landry, who was then the girlfriend (and now, wife) of Monteverde. Although she's a talented actress who is known for her co-starring role on the TV show *Eve*, the director insisted that she get no special consideration.

Instead, she took the time to prepare her own audition tape.

"And she knocked us out," says Serervino. "She had such emotional depth that we had no hesitation about casting her as Celia."

Packed into the tight twenty-four-day shooting schedule were numerous scenes in Manhattan, including the Mexican restaurant scenes which took place at Il Campanello on West 31st Street; José's family home, written as Long Island, was shot in Rockaway Beach, Bella Harbor, Queens; and the movie's early scenes which establish José as a soccer star were filmed in Greenpoint, Brooklyn.

Shooting at least six pages a day, which is twice that of a normal feature film pace, Monteverde encouraged his department heads to move briskly but creatively. Production designer Richard Lassalle not only helped establish the characters and environments with his artistic input and original ideas, but he gave every set his personal attention, including the colorful mural he painted in the restaurant.

"Looking back, I can say that this production was blessed," observes Pinckley. "I tried to anticipate the many obstacles that can get in your way, from weather problems to shooting in the crowded streets, but everything went incredibly smoothly."

With just two days of exteriors left to shoot, Monteverde did eventually come to a bump in the road. Not a drop of rain had fallen the previous weeks of shooting, but a storm hit the night before and it seemed certain that it would jeopardize two important exterior scenes in Brooklyn. "On Thursday, Denise had to break it to me that there was a 99 percent chance that it was going to rain the next day," recalls the director. "But the weather had been on our side for the whole shoot. So I said, let's come out tomorrow and shoot. But everyone thought I was crazy. So I woke up the next day and it was raining like mad. I drove to the set at 6:30 a.m., and here's our gaffer pointing to his computer and all the evidence that it would rain us out."

"We all stood on a corner with the rain dripping from trees, but the backyard where we wanted to shoot was relatively dry," recalls Pinckley. "So I ordered the crane that Alejandro had his heart set on."

"I was stubborn," admits Monteverde. "I looked up and I saw a hole in the sky—maybe the size of one airplane—and I'm thinking that this hole is going to stop over head and we're going to be able to shoot. Eduardo and Denise believed me. So we took a big leap of faith and set up. At 9:00 a.m. the rain stopped just two blocks away. If you had moved one block further in any direction, it would be raining. And according to the computers, it was even raining in our neighborhood. But we were dry until we finished shooting at 7:00 p.m., and then it started raining. It was a miracle. I would definitely call it a miracle."

At the end of the shoot, Monteverde returned to Los Angeles, where he teamed with editor Fernando Villena to find the visual, emotional story that the filmmakers wanted to tell. To compose the film's original score, Metanoia hired first-timer Stephen Altman, who not only wrote the music but personally performed each instrument himself before building a score that evokes hot salsa rhythms as well as quiet themes and intimate musical portraits.

The Actors

José, played by Eduardo Verástegui

Born and raised in Xicotencatl, Tamaulipas, a tiny village in Northern Mexico, Verástegui was the son of a sugar cane farmer. At the age of 18, he left his small town and headed to Mexico City to pursue a career in entertainment. Twelve years later, Eduardo had toured the world as a singer in the Mexican pop sensation Kairo and as an acclaimed solo recording artist, performing sold-out concerts in over thirteen countries.

Starring in five highly-rated Spanish soap operas for Televisa (broadcast in over nineteen countries), he has also been featured on hundreds of international magazine covers, including *People En Español*, which voted him one of the 50 Most Beautiful People. Verástegui has appeared opposite Jennifer Lopez in one of her most famous music videos "Ain't it Funny!" as well as in an international television commercial promoting her self-titled commercial fragrances.

In 2001, Verástegui was on a flight from Miami to Los Angeles when he was approached by the V.P. of Casting at 20th Century Fox for the studio's first-ever Latino-driven film, *Chasing Papi*, and won the starring role. He subsequently co-starred in an indie film called *Meet Me in Miami* and has appeared in such primetime television series as *CSI: Miami*, *Charmed*, and *Karen Cisco*.

In 2004, following an inspiration to transform his image, Verástegui left his agency and management and teamed with director Alejandro Monteverde and producers Sean Wolfington, Leo Severino, and Eustace Wolfington to make *Bella* and to form Metanoia

Films, a company committed to projects that entertain, engage, and inspire.

Nina, played by Tammy Blanchard

Blanchard's professional acting career started with a three-year stint as Drew Jacobs on CBS's daytime soap opera *Guiding Light*. Director Robert Ackerman then cast her to play the young Judy Garland in ABC's TV miniseries *Me and My Shadow: Life with Judy Garland*, which earned her much critical acclaim and an Emmy award for Best Supporting Actress. She co-starred with Blythe Danner in Lifetime's *We Were the Mulvaneys* and next to the Broadway stage in the latest revival of *Gypsy*, starring Bernadette Peters, directed by Sam Mendes. For her portrayal of Louise, Ms. Gypsy Rose Lee, she was nominated for the Tony and received a Theater World Award.

Blanchard joined Peter Falk for CBS's *When Angels Come to Town*, and in 2005, Robert DeNiro cast her in *The Good Shepherd* opposite Matt Damon and Angelina Jolie and scheduled for release in December of 2006. She most recently finished CBS's upcoming movie for television *Sybil*, where she plays the title role, starring with actress Jessica Lange.

Manny, played by Manny Perez

One of eleven siblings, he was born in a suburb of the city of Santiago in the Dominican Republic. At the age of 10, he and his family moved to the United States, settling in Providence, Rhode Island. He majored in drama at Marymount Manhattan College, graduating in 1992. He has also studied at the prestigious Ensemble

Studio Theatre and is a member of the Labryinth Theatre Company, in New York City.

Perez produced, starred, and co-wrote *Washington Heights*, an independent movie set in his own neighborhood. He starred in Sidney Lumet's critically acclaimed series "100 Center Street," NBC's *Third Watch* as Officer Santiago, and has appeared in such episodic shows as *Law & Order* and *CSI: Miami*. He will be seen in the upcoming films *El Cantante*, starring Marc Anthony and *Yellow*. At the Santo Domingo Invita: All-Star-Night at Radio City Music Hall, Perez was honored as one of the most prominent Dominican actors in the United States.

Celia, played by Ali Landry

Raised in a small Cajun town in Louisiana, Landry graduated from the University of Southwestern Louisiana with a degree in communications. She entered the Miss USA pageant in 1996 with the hope of launching a career in broadcasting or entertainment, and her win brought her to the attention of a major Hollywood talent agency. The popular host of such television shows as *Prime Time Comedy* and *America's Greatest Pets*, she eventually signed with Frito Lay for an acclaimed Doritos campaign that debuted during the 1998 Super Bowl telecast and gained her instantaneous fame.

Landry soon made the transition to acting with a variety of film and television roles, including a co-starring role in UPN's *Eve*, which has recently completed its third season. She has made guest-starring appearances on such episodic series as *Felicity*, *Pensacola*, and *Popular*. In 2000, she had a featured role in the motion picture *Beautiful*, directed by Sally Field.

About Metanoia Films

Bella is the first film produced by Metanoia Films. Our mission is to make movies that matter and have the potential to make a meaningful difference in people's lives. Metanoia is owned by Sean Wolfington, Eduardo Verastegui, Leo Severino, Alejandro Monteverde, and Eustace Wolfington. The team is brought together by a vision to make timeless films that make a positive difference in the world by promoting stories and characters that inspire and change people's lives. Metanoia Films has a number of projects in development, financed through a recently developed film fund.

Letter to the reader from the author

Dear Friend,

When my editor called me to tell me about *Bella* and ask whether or not I would consider writing the novelization of the screenplay, I was sitting in the waiting room of my dentist's office. I went out to the sunny front porch on that autumn afternoon and listened to the excitement in her voice as she told me about the movie, how it had won the People's Choice Award at the Toronto Film Festival and above all, how wonderful the *Bella* people were to talk with, how excited they were about their project and the message of faith, hope, love and life it gave to those blessed enough to see it. Did I want on board?

Of course! For years I've been a great lover of life in all its glorious, beautiful stages. From two cells to its dying breath, all life is a beautiful gift of God. We were on a tight time schedule by the time the writing process began. I had a month to turn the screenplay into a novel. Thankfully, the plot and dialogue were basically set, so I had the necessary time to deepen the characterization and provide the story of Nina's past, her hopes and dreams, her disappointments and trials. Leo Severino was so helpful in providing me with the ideas the writers weren't able to give screen time to and we hit the ground running, shooting emails and phone calls back and forth. It was a new process for me, but one I'm so glad to have had the opportunity to explore.

200

Thanks for picking up this book. I hope it blesses you, encourages you, and for some who find themselves in the valley of decision, that it will provide the light of hope.

Pax Christi,
Lisa
Lexington, KY

Reading Group Guide

1. José's grandmother often told him, "If you want to make God laugh, tell him your plans." In what ways did José's plans change throughout this story? And in what way did God get involved in José's plans and change them?

2. José is described as a good-looking man. Why do you think he now wears a long beard and shaggy hair? In what ways does that help him heal after the tragedy he caused?

3. José's name means "he will enlarge," and one of the meanings of the name Nina is "mother." In what ways do these character's names define their destiny?

4. Food is a significant part of this story. How did the flavors of the Mexican culture weave their way into the lives of the major characters—those with Hispanic heritage and those without?

5. Pieter is particularly cold to Nina when she discovers she is pregnant with his child. What motivates and informs his decisions in life? Why does he strive so much to "kiss up" to Manny?

6. Manny's restaurant is a successful, high-end establishment. He demands the absolute best from his employees and himself. Where does his drive come from and how has he become so successful? How does this influence his relationship with his brother?

7. Eduardo, Manny, and José are very distinct personalities. Take some time to compare them—what do they have in common?

8. How does Nina feel about her pregnancy, other than not being ready to mother a child? Is she embarrassed by her condition?

Does she worry about what others will think? Is she concerned at all about what her mother will think or say?

9. Celia clearly loved her daughter, Lucinda. And Lucinda's death was an earth-shattering tragedy for her. Do you think she will ever be ready to open lines of communication with José? How do you think she feels about the fact that José visits Lucinda's grave every morning?

10. José has, every day since the accident, lived with the guilt of killing Lucinda. It has changed his life in every way. At what level is Fernando also guilty of Lucinda's death? Celia?

11. Nina's father is described as a heavy drinker and inconsistent. But he is also someone who loved to have fun—scooping her up to dance the shag or take walks on the beach. Why is Nina so drawn to him in her memories? Does she think her life would be better now if he hadn't passed away?

12. When Nina first meets Maria, José's mother, she thinks: *This is what women should strive for. This is beauty far deeper than the skin, beauty that mirrors the heart.* How is Nina's longing—to be a good, kind, beautiful persona—exemplified in the story?